PRAISE FOR THE RULES

"A heart-thuddingly ner...

"Tense, suspenseful and explos... is a page-turner of the highest order." – Waterstones

"*The Rules* is a gulp-read with an addictive build-up of dread and a breathtaking finale." – Sue Wallman, author of *Dead Popular*

"[A] thought-provoking, hugely intelligent thriller that will stay with you long after you have read the last enigmatic line." – Mel Darbon, author of *Rosie Loves Jack*

"[A] page-turning, gripping, visceral thriller." – Chris Vick, author of *Girl. Boy. Sea.*

"[A] pulse-pounding new thriller… Elegant, nuanced characterisation interweaves thrilling action with moments of poignant emotion." – Imogen Russell Williams

"A truly addictive read." – Clair Bossons, Reading Zone

"A tense, challenging read, *The Rules* is one not to miss." – Sue Wilsher, North Somerset Teachers' Book Awards

"I was on the edge of my seat, always wondering what was coming next, right up until the explosive ending." – Jasmine Nightingale, Bookworm Reviewer

"A spine-tingling, gripping thriller!" – Emma Perry, My Book Corner

"Pacy, nerve-jangling reading – and with such a clever en... ...on."

For Tricia and Pete, who always seem to know which rules to follow and which to break.

The Rules contains content some readers may find triggering, including references to and instances of domestic abuse and violence, PTSD and panic attacks.

STRIPES PUBLISHING LIMITED
An imprint of the Little Tiger Group
1 Coda Studios, 189 Munster Road,
London SW6 6AW

www.littletiger.co.uk

First published in Great Britain by Stripes Publishing Limited in 2020
Text copyright © Tracy Darnton, 2020
Cover copyright © Stripes Publishing Limited, 2020
Additional images used under licence from Shutterstock.com
Author photograph © Charlie Matters

ISBN: 978-1-78895-214-9

A CIP ca[...]logue record for this book is available from the British Library.

Printed a[...]

FSC
www.fsc.org

The Fores[...] [...] a global, [...] [...]ion dedicated
to the pro[...] [...] [...]andards
based on [...]greed principles for responsible [...] [...] stewardship that are suppo[...]d by
environm[...]tal, social, and economic stakeholders. To learn more, visit www.fsc.org

10 9 8 7 6[...]

Tracy Darnton

LIVE BY

THE RULES

DIE BY

LITTLE TIGER

LONDON

Rule:
Trust No One

That's the strange thing about Dad's rules. I thought they were just his weird nonsense at first but then I realized I was following them. I mean, *choosing* to follow them – not just because he'd scratched them up on the massive board fixed to the wall. When Dad said *Trust no one*, he meant officials, the state, teachers, doctors, even other preppers.

And I followed the Rule.

I *still* follow the Rule.

I trust no one.

Especially him.

It's hard to imagine, but the Bowling Plaza is even worse than usual tonight. A giant, bobbing inflatable snowman is tethered to the roof, casting menacing shadows over the car park. Inside they've strung up cheap tinsel and 'Season's Greetings' banners, and a plastic tree with red and green baubles sits on the reception desk, getting in the way. It's only the first day of December, but already there's a sickly smell of stale mulled wine and a drunken office party is messing about by the pool tables.

Spotty Paul on shoe duty is dressed as an elf. You'd think he'd have more respect for himself. I don't like doing anything where you have to wear communal shoes. I've had enough of hand-me-down crap. Paul sprays them with a sickly aerosol between each customer, but even so, it freaks me out. I shudder as I put them on.

This interests Julie and she makes a note in her stripey book as usual.

"Maybe it's due to my feelings of abandonment," I tell her helpfully so she has something else to write down. "Or maybe it's because I dislike other people's smelly feet – which is completely rational, by the way."

Can you believe social services still has a budget for bowling and ice cream with Julie? The free ice cream would be OK if I was, like, six years old and on a beach. I'd rather have a double-shot Americano. I don't want a machine coffee in a plastic cup, so I stare for a while at the ice-cream choices to build the suspense before saying, "Nothing, thanks."

Julie looks disappointed. Maybe because she is now a grown woman licking a Solero next to a teenage girl sipping at a cup of water. I tell Julie she should cut back on the ice creams. If she takes all her clients out like this, no wonder.

"No wonder, Julie," I say, tutting.

Julie reddens and makes another note. Does she ever just call it as it is or does she always have some mumbo-jumbo excuse for my behaviour? "So who's drawn the short straw this year?" I ask.

"We're having a little trouble getting the right placement for you after term finishes," says Julie, fidgeting. This is Julie-speak for 'nobody wants you'.

"How will Santa know where to find me?" I stare, wide-eyed. I see her processing whether I'm serious or not. She just doesn't get irony.

To be honest, I see the Christmas stuff happening around me like a trailer for a film I don't get to watch in full; like those adverts on TV where one big happy family sits down at a glittering table with a shiny turkey. It's not my world. I'm like the Ghost of Christmas No One Wants in a foster home. They have to pretend to like me and cover up the fact their own child gets piles of gifts from relatives who actually give a damn.

"So no room at the inn," I say, and laugh. "That reminds me of something."

"It'll be fine." Julie pats my hand. I shrug her off.

"Tell them it's only dogs who aren't just for Christmas – you can get rid of kids, no problem," I say. "Anyway, I don't know what all the fuss is about. It's just a day when the shops are shut and the telly's better."

Julie's Solero is dripping down her hand. I watch as the drip plops on to her lap.

"Can't I stay at Beechwood by myself?" I already know the answer.

The office party's getting rowdier, singing along to piped Christmas singles from last century. Paul the elf has to intervene.

I start bowling with Julie. "The sooner we begin, the sooner it's over," I say.

We take the furthest alley as usual, like an old married

couple picking their regular table at the pizzeria.

I watch as she bowls. The ball trickles down the polished lane, heading slowly for the gutter at the side. She looks surprised. I don't know why. She's always rubbish at this. I used to think she was letting me win and hate her for it, as if my winning a game of ten-pin bowling would make everything all right in Julie-world. She keeps asking me if I'm OK, if I'm having a good time. Please! In this place? She's poking in her bag and casting glances my way like she's got more to tell me. I know the signs.

I win the game, by the way. I always win at things that don't matter.

"I have some news," says Julie, when we stop for her to take a rest and guzzle a fizzy drink.

Finally. What now?

"We've had a letter for you. From your dad. How do you feel about that?" She is obsessed, literally obsessed, with how I feel about everything. "We've struggled to find him, as you know. There was some confusion over names and information." She rummages in her briefcase and hands me an envelope. It sits in my hand like an unexploded bomb.

"If you don't want to look at it today, we can save it for another time. This must all be a big surprise," says Julie. She pats my knee. "Turns out he was back in America." She says it like that's an achievement – like he's a film star rather than a waster.

STRIKE! The teenagers on the alley next to us are doing

a moonwalk as the scoring machine flashes and plays loud music.

What am I doing in this place?

I look carefully at the envelope addressed to Somerset Social Services. The idiots looking for him must have told him where I've ended up. I flip it over. The return address is a place in Florida.

Julie checks her watch. Her concern for me only lasts until eight o'clock. She has to get back to her real life. She fiddles with her wedding ring.

I breathe. I listen to the clatter of the bowling balls and the whoops of another strike.

"OK," I say. "I'll read it."

I remove the letter from the envelope with my fingertips as if it's hot. It's oh-so-carefully typed, but I'm not fooled by him.

F.A.O. Amber Fitzpatrick

Dear Amber,

I can't tell you how pleased I was to finally have news of you. I'm sorry for your loss. I can only imagine what you've been through. But you don't need to worry about anything now – I'm here for you.

Your mom made it pretty difficult after we split

up, but I never stopped looking for the pair of you. You know I'd never give up. I went to your old addresses, but you'd moved on every time. You always were a hard girl to pin down, Amber. I can't wait to see what a beautiful young woman you've grown into.

I look forward to rekindling that special bond between us.

Your loving father

"Short but sweet," says Julie. "He's been looking for you all this time."

There's nothing sweet about my father, but then she's never met him. She knows nothing real about him. About him and me. I promised Mum in one of her lucid episodes that I'd never tell anyone what he used to do to her ... to me. He damaged her forever as sure as if he'd poured the alcohol and the pills down her throat himself. Some secrets are safer kept – especially when your dad's not the forgiving type.

It dawns on me that Julie's probably thinking Dad's the Christmas miracle, appearing to solve all her problems with placing me. She's seeing a happy reunion in Julie la-la land. But that's the last thing I want. And now he's found me, I know there's no way Julie can keep me safe. Not from him. I can't rely on anybody but me.

"So how do you feel about your dad getting back in touch?"

Feelings again. Always feelings.

She checks her notebook. "It's been a while since you've seen him. We had a lucky break in tracking him down at last."

Lucky? He's always landed on his feet. Like a cat with nine lives. After all Mum's efforts with fake names and addresses to make sure the do-gooders couldn't find him, even when she was in hospital and I was playing foster-care roulette.

"Would you like to write back?"

"No need," I say.

"You may feel that now," starts Julie, "but let's talk about it again when you've thought some more. Maybe chat it through with Dr Meadows. It's a lot to take in, sweetie."

And as usual she's got the wrong end of the stick. She hasn't actually read the letter properly. She doesn't know how my father operates – but I do. Ten days have passed since the posting date. He'll be on his way – if he's not already here. I look around me, suspicious now of the office partygoers. I need to make plans. I have to disappear.

"Now that your mum is…" Julie pulls awkwardly at her necklace.

"Dead, you mean."

"…no longer here, we could explore other family options."

Family? My dad? I'd rather be shacked up with some cardboard and a blanket in a multi-storey car park. Mum and I did it to get away from him before. And yet now … now I have more to lose. I have what Julie would call prospects. My grades are good, I want to go to university. I have decent teachers. Not that I'd ever tell them that.

Julie puffs to her feet and waddles over to choose a bowling ball. "Come on, double or quits."

I think of my neat little room at Beechwood School: the duvet cover that Julie and I picked out at Primark, the posters I carefully stuck to the wall and the row of books on the shelf. There's a bright orange cushion Julie bought me for my birthday that I pretended not to like. Too big to pack now. The furniture is brown and slightly tatty, circa 1999, but everyone's room is like that. I don't stand out among the boarders except in the holidays.

Julie heads off to the ladies after all that Diet Coke, while I stare at the wall and try to think straight. I thought I'd made myself invisible, and then Julie's boss ruins it all by interfering in my business. The letter has tracked me down like a heat-seeking missile and I'm not free of Dad even at the rundown Bowling Plaza. I dig my fingernails into the palm of my hand, cross with myself for getting complacent, for getting to like somewhere, when I should have known it wouldn't last.

Julie hugs me in the car once we've pulled up outside Beechwood. I let her. She won't be seeing me again. I bite my lip and stare out at the flickering lights on the tree by the main entrance. The angel at the top has broken and the wings are blinking on and off. I was going to help decorate the hall with holly and ivy next week. Proper greenery from the garden – real decorations, not ones made of foil and plastic.

She reaches over to the back seat and passes me a red envelope. Not another letter bombshell.

"It's an advent calendar," she says, smiling.

It's bigger than a normal greetings card, with twenty-four tiny windows scattered across a picture of polar bears wearing knitted scarves. Silver glitter falls off as I touch it. Merry Christmas, Planet.

"Where are the chocolates, Julie?" I say. "Did you eat them all?"

Her cheeks flush as she ignores my comment. "Open it up, lovely."

Inside, Julie's written in her best handwriting:

Dear Amber, Hope you enjoy opening the windows and are looking forward to the festive season. J xxx

She never quite has the right words. Never sounds normal. Because she fools herself that she's 'down with the kids', she's added a smiley face. Why would I be looking forward to the festive season, when we've already established it's a major inconvenience finding somewhere for me to go?

"It feels like snow's on the way," says Julie, as I stare down at the polar bears. "A white Christmas maybe."

A cold one, then.

"Could I have some extra cash?" I ask. "I need some toiletries and stuff."

She marks it in her notebook and hands me thirty pounds.

"I'll see you next week. We can write a response to your dad's letter together, if you like. No pressure. Whatever's best for you." She smiles. "Maybe with Christmas coming…"

She's happier being useful, making plans.

"Sure. I'll think about it." I shove the cash in my pocket and toss her a bone: "I know I can be a right cow sometimes."

She blushes, unsure what to say to that as it's so true. I can't help but feel slightly fond of her and her flowery smocks.

"Take care of yourself," she says.

I intend to.

"We'll sort something out for you, I promise. Don't forget your advent calendar."

Julie tucks my hair behind my ear.

I get out of the car and lean down towards the window. I nearly say something. I nearly say, 'Thanks, I know you want to help, it's not your fault'. I nearly tell her how I really feel and ask for help, but I can't quite do it. The weight of all that's happened is pushing on my chest. So instead I tap on the glass.

"Go easy on the mince pies, Julie," I say.

I turn and walk away.

———

When I get back to my room, I pull out my rucksack from under the bed. It's my Grab-and-Go Bag, for escape in the event of catastrophe. Dad would be proud of me. *Always have your Grab-and-Go Bag.* That's the Rule.

I pull out my emergency plan, my hands shaking slightly. It's short. Options in the event of imminent disaster are to stay put and fortify, or bug out and go. I choose the second. I'll be well away from Dad if he turns up here at Beechwood. My plan has the address of an empty holiday cottage hundreds of miles away in Northumberland and how to get there. It belongs to Phil and Sue, foster carers from when Mum was in hospital. I can't go back to any of the places we used to live in Somerset or Wales – either Dad already knows them or he could easily find out now. Our last home, the farm, I'm *never* going back there. Phil and Sue's place, The Haven, is somewhere I came to *after* that life with Dad ended. And even if he manages to get hold of information from social services, a holiday home would never have been recorded in the chaos of my file.

I retrieve the cash I've stashed; notes pressed carefully

inside my hardback edition of *The Handmaid's Tale*. I've been picking up money from the more careless sixth formers who don't lock up their rooms properly. My contingency fund. I write a note for Mrs Maz the relief matron, signing it from Julie. I say that I'm on an unexpected weekend visit to old foster parents and will be back in time for school on Monday morning.

Phones are too easily traced so I switch mine off and wedge it at the back of my drawer. There's no one I need to call. No one who will be worried about me except in a purely professional capacity. I have a brief pang of concern for Julie – she might get into trouble or might genuinely worry about me. But she'll get over it.

Some of the people here are the closest things to friends I've had for a while, but let's get real: I won't be missed. I've been hanging out with Sophie mostly. A girl who's been chucked out of some of the best schools in Britain, smokes twenty a day without anyone ever catching her and can swear in her posh, little-girl voice in a way that cracks me up. She's taken on the job of filling in the gaps in my cultural education and I try to show interest in the Netflix shows she wants to talk about. She'll find a new project after I'm gone.

I scan my room for anything else I want to take. I'm not big on clothes. Sophie jokes that I look like an undertaker's apprentice because I wear so much black. The fact that I rarely smile probably has something to do with it too.

I like being the girl who doesn't stand out, the girl nobody notices. Being inconspicuous can keep you alive. I tie my hair in a low ponytail, put on a beanie hat and add a big scarf that can cover half my face. I pack my decent waterproofs and wear my usual black coat with a deep hood. I don't want to look like I'm walking in the mountains – I'm just a teenage girl catching a train to family. Normal. Average.

At the last minute, I pick up Julie's advent calendar. I open the first window to reveal a tiny 'Letter to Santa'. Ironic. Dad's letter came with the major implication that I am on the naughty list, for being quite so difficult to find. Thanks to him, I've now got no idea where I'll be by the time the rest of the cheap, glittery card windows are open.

I shouldn't bring the advent calendar. It serves no purpose.

I pack it in my bag.

⎯⎯⎯

Thirty minutes' brisk walk gets me to the station. I need to think ahead, that's one of the Rules: think how this will look to anyone trying to find me. I buy two tickets, exactly as set out in my emergency plan. First, I get a single to Cardiff from the bored man at the counter, using my bank card. Julie knows about my bank account – she helped me set it up. I make a meal of it, spending ages looking for my purse, asking inane questions about things to visit there so that he's more likely to remember me. I buy a second ticket for Edinburgh from the machine out of sight of the counter, feeding notes carefully into the slot. My dad came to think all state authorities were out to get him, tracking his movements, prying into his finances and his irregular immigration status. So I'm well trained in concealing my data trail. Or laying a fake one.

I wait for the train in the ladies' toilets, away from any platform cameras. I dive into a cubicle when a woman enters – and then tell myself not to be so jumpy, to pull myself together, not to draw attention. No one is coming to take me back to school. As my train finally pulls in to the platform, I merge with other passengers and hop on, hood up. I change platforms at Bath, tagging along behind a noisy group of tourists and their wheelie cases.

Pulling into London past midnight, I spend hours drifting between rundown 24-hour fast-food places to keep warm while I wait for the first train north. I don't use a bank card, just cash, and only if I'm getting the evils from the staff and have to buy something to stop them kicking me out into the cold. This cash has to last me. I drink fizzy drinks and strong coffee to stay awake to keep an eye on my stuff.

It's easier to do all this if you've trained your whole life for it. But I need to add a new worst-case scenario to the list of emergency events we planned for – not one Dad ever mentioned. *Running from him.*

RULE:
PREP FOR THE WORST

The Scouts have a similar rule, but their motto *Be Prepared* is more about cake sales than hardcore survivalist plans. They are a lightweight organization compared to us. Our Rule was about being prepared for the very worst that life can throw at you. *Prepared. Not scared.* Other kids in Year 3 could list dinosaurs or football players. I could rattle off SHTF scenarios. That's Shit Hits the Fan to the uninitiated. Turns out, it wasn't a topic wholly suitable for show-and-tell.

First, the bad language got me into trouble, with or without an acronym. Then the Shit really did Hit the Fan.

It was my go right after Charlotte, who talked about her rabbit, which was unfortunate timing. Maybe I shouldn't have said that Charlotte's rabbit would be put straight into a casserole if the shit hit. Maybe I shouldn't have opened up my Swiss Army knife to demonstrate how I would skin Charlotte's rabbit. You see, Dad and I were preparing for many things:

War

Civil unrest

Chemical explosion

Fuel shortages

We were preppers. Survivalists. People prepared to do what it took to survive. To sacrifice the odd pet rabbit.

Bio-terrorism

Forest fires

Water contamination

Banking system collapse

Giant solar flares

I was proud of my dad then. I thought he was so much smarter than everyone else's father because he knew all about how we'd survive while the world was ending around us.

Flooding

Cyber attack

Power outage

Asteroid strike

At that time, when I was in junior school, Dad came and left our lives as he wished. Probably running back to the US to sponge some more money off his mom in Ohio. The grandma I never met. I imagined her baking cookies and apple pies in a wooden house with a wide porch and a swing. The reality was probably rather different. She did raise my dad after all.

Spanish flu

Bird flu

Swine flu

Of course, I was an idiot. No excuses. I thought one day Dad would take us with him back to the States to meet my cookie-baking grandma and we'd live next to Disneyland, maybe *in* Disneyland, in the Sleeping Beauty castle and every day would be perfect. So why wouldn't I show off my Grab-and-Go Bag and recite the list of impending disasters I'd learned from him?

Pandemic

Ebola

Post-antibiotic resistance

Civil unrest

My teacher was pulling nervously at her collar. Her liberal belief in free expression was grappling with the need to avoid lifelong trauma for a bunch of seven-year-olds. Not to mention the letters of complaint. A red flush slowly spread from her chest up her neck and across her cheeks until finally she tried to intervene.

Earthquake

Tsunami

Alien invasion

Electromagnetic pulse

As I got older, I came to see that Dad *wanted* something

bad to happen. So that he'd be proved right. The guys down the pub who laughed at him for spending his money on a gas mask would suffocate to death before his very eyes. All his paranoid fantasies would be vindicated. So what if most people would be doomed? *We'd* be sitting in a cabin in the woods eating pickles and canned fish, Dad grinning from ear to ear and saying, "I told you so."

Though by then he would probably only have communicated in giant, angry capital letters: I TOLD YOU SO.

Crop failure
Nuclear war
Drought
Zombie apocalypse

You might think that only a complete psychopath would want an actual emergency, a real disaster. And you'd be right.

I was never going to get the train all the way to Edinburgh, of course. I sleep in the safety of my train seat against the window and set my alarm for three hours, my arms wrapped round my bag. I get off at Newcastle, helping a family with their buggy like I'm the big sister. They offer me a lift in their taxi and I take it, rammed in the back of a mini cab that reeks of air freshener. The toddler leans against me, head nodding and dribbling down my coat. I tell them I'm a student at the uni and they drop me at my 'house share'. I stand waving at the gate of a random house until the cab turns the corner, heave my bag on to my back and stride off towards the main road.

Going to the Bowling Plaza feels like weeks ago but it was less than twenty-four hours. I'm queasy and shaky from lack of sleep and treat myself to a bacon sandwich at a shabby café with no CCTV. I'm being overcautious but hey, I can't help myself. It's ingrained. Mental attitude is what distinguishes a survivor. Self-reliance, doing what you have to do on little sleep. I have to stay switched on until I reach the safety of Phil and Sue's place.

I cadge a lift further towards The Haven with a Latvian lorry driver who's only passing through. Perfect. He listens to heavy metal music, not the local radio stations. He'll be long gone before anyone starts looking for me. If they even bother. It took social services six months to find some of my paperwork once, so I expect they'll be behind the curve in tracking me down. The police won't be interested. I'm nearly an adult, voluntarily going walkabout for a while. No big deal.

Dad is a different matter. I've avoided him successfully for more than two years. I let myself believe that he'd gone for good. I should have known that with Dad, it's never over.

The lorry driver drops me at a layby on the A1. I check my map and choose to walk the last three miles, dodging out of sight if a car passes. I don't want a lift from a chatty local. The rucksack is tight and heavy on my back. I'm obsessive about making sure nothing rattles. That no one ever hears me coming.

Bamburgh is quiet and bleak out of season. Last time I was here it was the school holidays. We walked along the coast, visited the castle, ate fish and chips. I gave Phil and

Sue a hard time but I guess they were all right. They'll have a new batch of kids now, crammed in the bunk beds in the back bedrooms down in Somerset.

I take the turning down Beach Lane. Two cats scrap on the road over a torn rubbish bag. The Haven is the last place on the right. It's a bungalow with grey pebble-dashed walls and a paved front garden, weeds thriving in the cracks around pots of dead plants. It's not exactly a cutesy holiday home but they'd rent it sometimes in the summer to friends who'd left it too late to find anything good.

The house is closed up, curtains drawn, but I walk slowly round it, peering in, just to make sure. A pile of junk mail lies on the mat inside the glass porch. A key box with a pad code is tucked round by the wheelie bin. Phil was terrible at remembering passwords and PIN numbers so everything in his life was 1066 – the burglar alarm, the cash machine (useful to know, for a tenner every now and then) *and* the holiday cottage key box. He won't have had the imagination to change it, I'm certain. There's nothing worth nicking here anyway. It belonged to his dead mum and is still full of brown old-lady furniture.

I tap in 1066 and the box clicks open. The keyring says 'World's Best Husband'. Phil and Sue were into all that schmaltzy stuff – Valentine bears and greetings cards. As though all the love stuff would rub off on the rest of the household – damaged kids like me who scowled at them across the kitchen table. It didn't.

The key's shiny, newly cut, and I fiddle with it in the lock before it works. I step over the post and head for the kitchen at the back. Even once I've pulled up the blind, the room is still dingy. I switch on the lights – a fluorescent strip blinking on, dead flies silhouetted in the casing. It's musty, except for the overpowering diffuser by the door – a smell like disinfectant lemons. I turn on the heating and open the windows to let out the stale air. It doesn't take me long to check all the rooms. The cottage is much smaller and tattier than I remember. I guess places seem bigger on sunny days, better when you're on an actual holiday rather than just finding somewhere to lie low.

I fantasize occasionally that I can escape the past, that I can change my identity, shed my old skin and emerge as a different person. But it's just a fantasy. That kind of change isn't easy. I prop up the advent calendar on a shelf in the kitchen and open the second door. A sprig of holly. Prickly like me. Maybe that could be a new identity: Holly. I'd fit right in with the Millie, Molly, Izzy brigade at school.

I finally sit down, exhausted and shaky. The Haven is as safe a house as I can make it. The adrenaline's beginning to drain away. I'm in a place I hoped I'd never have to use and I don't know how long I'll be here. My emergency plan doesn't help. I wrote *until I know it's safe to return to Beechwood* – but what if it never is? What then? I'm meant to stay one step ahead. That's the Rule. I guess I'm out of practice.

I need to keep my strength up. Sue always kept basic supplies up here and I help myself to a lunch of canned vegetable soup and rice pudding, warming them in the dented saucepan on the hob, before my head starts to nod and I drag myself upstairs to crash out for a few hours in the half-remembered back bedroom.

RULE:
LEAVE NO TRACE

Loud music woke me up. I cautiously padded into the lounge, pulling on a jumper. Mum was kneeling by the wall of Rules with a bucket of water and a scrubbing brush. I dimly recognized the music from when I was little – from a time when it was just me and Mum and she used to scoop me up and dance around the kitchen with music on full blast. She'd make up a reason for a party:

It's Friday.

It's a 'let's finish tidying up' party.

It's an 'I've been paid today' party.

I didn't really care about *why*. I just loved that we were dancing in the kitchen and that Mum was making popcorn in the big saucepan. The kernels fired against the metal lid in a series of pops as the oil heated up. She shook the saucepan from time to time to stop it sticking and then she'd lift the lid to reveal overflowing fluffy popcorn. To a five-year-old it was magic. She divided out the popcorn between the two of us and scattered icing sugar through a tiny sieve, like a snowstorm. I'd lick my fingers and wipe them round the empty dish to pick up the last sweet dregs.

But there was no smell of popcorn now. No party. Just blaring music and a sobbing woman. A snippet of music from a decade ago couldn't get us back there, away from this.

Away from him.

Mum's face was red and blotchy from crying. A bruise on her left cheekbone spread up towards her eye. Her tears were streaking through the foundation she'd plastered on to cover it.

"Let's get rid of it all, Amber. Let's rub the Rules away and everything will be all right, won't it?"

She scrubbed at the board, water dripping down her arm and on to the carpet, the words blurring and mixing into a mess of smeary white clouds across the wall. Dad shouted from upstairs about the noise. His heavy steps began descending the stairs. I couldn't fix this. Mum smiled at me. Not a proper smile. Just someone forcing their mouth into a shape.

"See, Amber. They've gone. I did it."

December

5

I'm getting used to living at The Haven. I have a new routine of runs along the coast and dunes, trying to clear my head of my past with Dad, and solitary meals in front of the TV. I know I'm killing time, that I need to think ahead, but this is the best I can manage right now. The Haven's not exactly 'home' – I don't really know what that would feel like any more – but I'm pleased to see it when I turn back up the lane. Maybe that's the most I can ever expect.

The ginger-haired guy at the corner shop nods in recognition when he sees me now. Yesterday he commented on the weather. Today he tried to chat, asked where I was staying. I was non-specific. "Oh, you know, in one of the holiday cottages, belongs to my nan." *Trust no one.* That was the Rule. He smiles but that doesn't mean he's a good guy. I should have kept it simple. Now I've invented a nan he might want to ask about. Stupid. I replay the conversation in my head, telling myself not to worry. I'm safe here. I should switch to another shop tomorrow – the one attached to the petrol station. It's further away but a bored shift worker won't ask me any questions.

I stick my shopping in the fridge and put the kettle on. I spread out the newspaper on the table, switch on the radio. I could carry on living here like this until I know Dad has given up and gone back to the States. I half regret ditching my phone. I could have called Sophie, sworn her to secrecy and asked if he'd come looking for me at school yet. Except I'm not that stupid. No contact is the safest way. But the longer I'm here, the harder it'll be to pick up that life. And I don't want to admit it, but if Dad finds out I go to Beechwood, it'll never be safe to go back.

I work through the newspaper, checking all the columns, seeing if there's a flicker of a news story on me. It's been two days since the penny must have dropped with Mrs Maz; she will have called Julie. They've probably had lots of meetings. How long before they think I may be at risk and the police go public?

I don't have a mother to do a sobbing TV appeal, flanked by a doting husband and a family liaison police officer. Maybe Julie would say something. "This is so out of character for Amber (LIE). Amber, if you're out there, please get in touch. We're all worried about you (LIE). You're not in any trouble (LIE)."

Is being my substitute sobbing relative in Julie's job description? Perhaps she'll have media training, get a new dress from Rent-a-Tent on expenses.

I close the paper. I'm not in there.

My eyes flick up to the advent calendar. How many days have I been here? I didn't open it at breakfast but there's a new little picture on the bottom left – a gingerbread man with red icing buttons and a fixed smile.

I jump up and look quickly around the ground floor, my heart beating faster. There's a scruffy bag and a green parka jacket in the back porch. The floorboards above me creak and someone flushes the toilet.

I head for the front door but, as I reach for the handle, a young man in sweatpants and a crumpled T-shirt is coming down the stairs.

"Hey, Goldilocks. Who's been sleeping in my bed?" he says.

As he gets to the bottom step, I grab him by his shirt and force my weight against his chest, rolling him over on to the floor and pinning him down. I force his chin up with the flat of my palm, holding his head to the floor and sit astride him.

"Who the hell are you?" I ask.

"Ow. Get the fuck off me!" He's got muddy-brown hair and seems my age or a little older. It's hard to tell exactly – he's got a scrappy beard and acne scars. He's tall but thin – not strong enough to overpower me, not from this position.

But I'm not taking any chances and I increase my force on his head. My mind's whirring – I've seen him before but can't place him.

"I asked you a question," I say. "Who are you? Why are you here?"

"Josh," he squeezes out. "I'm Josh Atkins. Just crashing here. Can you let me get up now?"

I stand slowly. The name rings a bell. I study his face as he sits cautiously on the stairs and rubs his chin. "That's quite a set of moves you've got there. Are you Special Forces or something?" He smiles nervously at me, revealing a cracked front tooth. Not my handiwork.

"Wait, I *know* you. You're –" he clicks his fingers while he thinks – "Amber! That's it – Amber," he says. "We overlapped for a few weeks at Phil and Sue's. A couple of years ago probably. We called you Amber Warning. Not so you'd hear us. We didn't have a death wish."

"Who's 'we'?"

"Me and Diggo. You decked him for looking at you funny over the Weetabix one morning. You weren't one of the friendliest kids, putting it mildly. I got your necklace back off Diggo when he nicked it. Remember?"

My hand goes to Mum's locket round my neck. I *do* remember. It was one of the few nice things anyone did for me in a blurry mess of a time when Mum was back in hospital. I keep her close, but I took the tiny photo of Dad out long ago.

"Phil and Sue, eh? So we're practically related. Truce?" He holds out a hand. "Er, this is where you say sorry for wrestling me to the floor and nearly breaking my neck."

"I just reacted," I say. "You could have been a burglar. Don't surprise me in future." I don't want anyone else here, but I don't want him complaining about me either. I take the easiest path and help him up.

"Crap apology accepted," he says. "I've had a lot worse. Get any decent food on your trip out?" He edges into the kitchen, taking care not to come too close to me, and opens the fridge.

I lean by the door, ready for a speedy exit, watching him all the time.

He gets mugs from the cupboard above the kettle and a couple of teaspoons from the drawer. He knows his way around the kitchen. "Tea?"

I nod. I'm unsettled. I'd been thinking of this place as mine and here's someone who treats it like it's his.

"Going to tell me why you're here?" he asks. He tosses teaspoons on to the table. Randomly. "And why you're so jumpy?"

"Just passing," I say, neatening up the spoons.

"Yeah, right." He smirks. "Because this place is dead handy." He squeezes the teabag and pushes my mug towards me across the table, still wary of me.

I glare at him as he dunks custard creams, *my* custard creams, into his tea.

He shrugs. "I'll start then, shall I? I like to crash here every now and then. Especially when it's as cold as this week. I can catch up on the personal hygiene front." He sniffs his armpit. "Ahh, sweet. You should have seen me when I got here."

I say nothing.

"Fine. Not very chatty, are you?" He retrieves his bag and empties out some screwed-up clothes. "I'm going to put a wash on," he says. "Want me to bung in anything of yours?"

"With *your* stuff?" I'm too slow to stop a look of disgust crossing my face. I can smell the clothes from here.

"All right, point taken. I've been trying an experiment in self-cleansing that kind of works with my hair but not with the jeans." He whistles as he tries to sort his clothes by colour but then thinks better of it and shoves the first pile into the machine.

"Look at us, all domesticated," he says. "If Phil and Sue could see us now, eh? Have you kept in touch?"

"How long are you staying?" I ask coldly.

"How long are *you* staying?"

"Shouldn't it be first come, first served?"

"In that case, I win. Because I was here last month too." He taps his pocket. "Got myself an extra set of keys cut. We could always phone up Phil and ask him what he thinks." He winks. "No? Thought not. Tell you what, you can keep the back bedroom this time, even though I usually have that one myself. I'll take the front. I'll be gone shortly. Probably. Where are you living these days? Got another foster family?"

"I'm at, *was* at, boarding school. They have a few places for kids like me. I didn't do well in foster care."

Slight understatement.

"I bet. Diggo probably got off lightly. But you don't kick off there? At this school? What did you say it was called?"

"I didn't." It's nothing to do with him. I'm not going to explain that I like being at school, I like the teachers who encourage me. I like my little study bedroom. I like talking about unreliable narrators in the Lit Discussion Group. I like pretending that I can have that life. But if I'd stayed, Dad could have come marching in there and dragged me back to our past. Julie and her stripey notebook would have *helped* him to do it. He'd have fooled the lot of them into thinking he was a normal father and I'd have been put on a plane to the US with him before his charms had worn off.

Josh helps himself to a yogurt, which he shovels in, standing by the open fridge door. "What are you doing up here then? Term's not over, is it?" he asks between mouthfuls.

"I fancied a holiday."

"Yeah, right."

"It's complicated," I say, hoping to shut him down.

"Things are only complicated if you let them be," he says.

"That's crap."

"Go for the simple life."

"Is that what yours is? Looks great," I say. "There's Keep Fit in the village hall tomorrow and a Christmas craft fayre to look forward to on Saturday."

He tilts his head to one side and waves his spoon in my direction. "I'm sensing a certain amount of sarcasm and animosity. Chill."

I hate people, usually of the male gender, telling me to chill, to smile more, to cheer up, it may never happen. I clench and relax my fist repeatedly in my pocket to let the anger subside.

Josh shouldn't be here.

Having company wasn't in the plan.

RULE:
USE YOUR WEAKNESS AS YOUR STRENGTH

I guess not every teenager is trained in hand-to-hand combat.

Martial arts have a code, respect between fighters. But Dad wanted me to fight dirty. To win at all costs. To be able to fight off the marauding hordes of people swarming over our house to get their hands on a tin of sardines. We watched YouTube videos where some deranged guy with a long grey beard in Montana would demonstrate how to kill a zombie. Dad was showing me all sorts of horrors. Meanwhile, other kids at school were excited if they got into a 15-rated movie at the cinema.

"It's kill or be killed, Amber, honey," he'd say, gripping me in a headlock while I thrashed uselessly. I knew he meant other people. But all the same, some part of my brain wondered if it would ever be down to him and me, fighting over the last ration pack. I wondered how much his 'blood is thicker than water' mantra and the need to preserve his gene pool (me) would count over his selfish need to preserve himself. That's what all this was always about. But sharing a gene pool doesn't mean you automatically love – or even *like* – someone.

I paid attention to his lessons. He called them training. He had a clipboard and a stopwatch. I learned how to strike an attacker so as to instantly break their nose, where to cut their throat. I practised thrusting my fingers into grapes to desensitize myself from poking actual eyeballs, bit pastrami that had the texture of a tongue. I knew how to force my arms up and away to shrug off an attacker from behind, how to stamp on their feet, kick shins, twist testicles. I could use a set of keys between my fingers like a street fighter's knuckle-duster.

"Use your weakness as your strength. That's the Rule. They won't expect you to be able to do all this," said Dad. "You'll have the element of surprise. If someone's got you pinned to the floor with his trousers round his ankles and his hands on your wrists, you're ready to bite his tongue. Don't hesitate. Play dirty. Play real dirty, Amber."

These are confusing messages for a thirteen-year-old. Seeing all other people as a potential threat to your own safety and existence messes with your head. So the next time there was an incident at school, I may have slightly overreacted. Ben from Year 11 thought it was funny to lift up my skirt with the tip of his hockey stick, and got more than he bargained for. I saw red. Massive fiery clouds of red. I'd been walking around like a pressure cooker set to explode from Dad being back in our lives again. And I just flipped.

Dad was right about the unexpected though. No one expected me to do what I did. Ben ended up slumped against the lockers with his nose broken and bleeding. He didn't know which to clutch first, his nose or his bruised balls. Thing was, I could barely remember attacking him.

I ran to the girls' toilets and locked myself in a cubicle. My hands were quivering. Not a mark on them though. Not a bruise. I wiped off the splattered specks of Ben's blood with toilet paper and flushed it away. I thought one of the teachers would be sure to come and find me and haul me up in front of the Head, suspend me, report me to the police. All those scenarios were spinning through my mind, playing out in various shades of worry. But the time ticked on. I watched feet come and go. Toilets flushed, doors banged. I gingerly came out, washed my hands, threw cold water over my face. I stared back at the girl in the broken mirror with puffy eyes that I barely recognized. She was capable of a brutal assault on the spin of a second. Was that what Dad was turning me into?

I got grudging respect from the boys in Year 11 afterwards. They'd sing out 'Wonder Woman' when I went past – sniggering and poking fun at Ben. His version of events was that he'd 'had an accident' with his hockey stick 'on a slippery floor'. I don't know whether anyone believed it but I wasn't saying anything different. Sexism was alive and kicking and he was ashamed he'd been beaten *by a girl*. And a weedy-looking one from Year 8 at that.

What I learned:

Injured noses bleed a lot.

Ben was not a feminist.

Dad was right. Like so many of his Rules were proving to be.

My weakness was my strength.

December
6

The advent calendar door sticks this morning. I dig at it with my nail and I'm annoyed when I rip it slightly. It's an angel: plump and glowing golden. No way her wings would hold her up. Basic aerodynamics. And why are angels always white and blond?

Josh's phone (old-style brick) is charging on the worktop. Josh the sloth is still in bed. His phone is not even locked. I scroll through his contacts and recent history. He has even fewer friends than me, and he's not been in contact with anyone recently.

It crossed my paranoid mind earlier that he could have been sent by my dad. So I checked through his room last night while he was doing the washing-up but found nothing of any interest. Literally nothing. He has barely any stuff.

I put his phone down but then pick it up again. Should

I call Julie, say I'm OK? Explain, and hope she rides in to save me in her white Hyundai. But it's never going to be that simple – there are procedures they have to follow. They cannot break a rule. Dad can be charming, convincing. There's no query about him at all on the record.

I swore to Mum I wouldn't ever tell the social workers about what happened. She was adamant about it – partly her shame that we'd be judged, partly her fear that we'd suffer consequences. I get that. I feel it too. Feelings are hard to subdue, to rationalize.

Mum felt it reflected on her, made her look bad, that she'd left me with him when she tried to sort herself out. And the last couple of times I saw her, she basically apologized for ever sleeping with him in the first place and making him my dad. But that was like saying that half of me was a cancerous growth she wished she could cut out. When she saw *me*, she saw *him*. Whatever I do, he'll always be a part of me. That's a scary thought in the middle of the night.

Am I mad to be keeping that promise to Mum? Julie's number is written on a card in my purse. I trace the digits for a minute or two, pondering where the balance of truth and lies would fall between me and Dad. I tap in the number but my finger hovers over the call button. In my head, I replay Julie's voice stumbling its way through the recorded message – I've heard it often enough. I'm going to do it, honestly. But then I'm paralyzed by that promise to Mum. It was the only thing I had to offer her at the end.

I can't just let it go. I can't let Mum down like that. And the cold, hard truth is that I'm the only one who can keep me safe.

I don't make the call, instead replacing the phone exactly where it was. I've got a feeling in the pit of my stomach I don't recognize. Homesickness? Do I miss *Julie*? Don't be idiotic. No one would miss Julie. I play with my locket, pulling it along the chain from left to right and back to the centre again.

I check my kit to calm me down. I get out my map to familiarize myself with the area in case I have to bail. I want to suss out the quiet roads on foot, how far I can get. But before I can look at it properly, Josh thuds down the stairs singing a Christmas tune. I don't know how he wakes up so cheerful. He has nothing to be cheerful about. From the cut on his cheek, he's shaved and tidied up his beard. It looks thinner, neater.

"Now I get why you're here," he says, peering over my shoulder at the map. I can smell his toothpaste breath. "You're doing a Duke of Edinburgh expedition and you got lost?"

"Funny. Very funny. If ever communications fail, at least I'll know one end of a map from the other and—"

"If communications fail? You *are* Special Forces." He's laughing at me.

There's a clattering noise behind me. He's poking in my bag, fishing out the sleeping bag and the camping stove.

I stand up. "What the hell! That's mine. Put. It. Down."

"What do you have in here? Fish hooks and line, matches, first-aid kit..." He pulls out the folding mini-shovel. "What's this? Planning a spot of gardening?" He unfolds it and turns it in his hand.

"It's the poo shovel," I say. "For digging a latrine."

He drops it instantly and it clatters on the tiled floor. "Yuk! Tell me it's unused?" He wipes his hands on his jeans. "Hardcore camping. I'm more of a static caravan kind of guy."

"Can you get off my stuff, or..."

"Uh-oh. Am I getting the Amber Warning? Going to take me out with a rolled-up sleeping mat or a spork?" He's smiling at me. "I'm on your side, Amber. Whatever. We were both at Phil and Sue's."

"You keep saying that. So what? That makes us siblings, does it?"

"It makes us *something*," he says. "It means something to me."

He cups his hands round his face. "Look – I'm adorable. Who wouldn't want to adopt me as a big brother? Though..." The smile goes. "Your school knows you're on your little holiday, right? No one's going to think I've whisked you off, are they?"

"Of course not. I just need to get my head together for a few days, sort something out and then I'm going back. They'll barely know I'm gone."

"Because I don't want any trouble, Amber. People don't tend to believe blokes like me. You know that."

"There won't be any trouble, OK. No one knows I'm here. Anyway, I'll be off out of your way at some point. That's what the map's for. I won't be your problem."

"What do you have to sort out way up here that you can't sort at Hogwarts?"

I sigh heavily. There's no reason to sugar-coat it for him. "My dad's a psycho. He's back in the country and I don't want to see him. End of story. I'm not a child, am I?"

"You're not eighteen though – are you?"

I shrug. "Nearly. What's a couple of months?"

"If you say so." He pushes the mini-shovel towards me with his toe. "Now tell me why you're ready to dig a toilet." He folds his arms and stands waiting for my answer.

I take a breath. I haven't explained this to anyone at Beechwood, where I kept my bag shoved far back underneath my bed. There's been no need. I hide my past as best I can from my classmates, from Julie, the authorities. But Josh – he's like me, navigating a path of self-preservation away from his past. He's on the outside too. And I remember him as the guy who got Mum's locket back for me. Maybe if I tell him a tiny part, he'll quit with the questions.

"My dad's a prepper. A survivalist," I say. "He's preparing for the existential threat he thinks is just around the corner. Preparing for any 'shit hits the fan' scenarios. He trained me up from a little kid." I pull out a couple of bin bags from under the sink. "*You* see a black bin bag to use in the dustbin. *I* see a 'prep' – rapid shelter, waterproofing, insulation if I fill it with hay or dry leaves. It's a basic emergency substitute for my actual Grab-and-Go Bag that you looked in. I always used to have two bin bags with me – even if I was only going out for a couple of hours. But I've been managing trips out with Julie, my social worker, for months now without sneaking them along."

"OK. You're convincing me that prepping is slightly weird."

"You can use a bin bag to carry commandeered supplies…" I continue.

"That sounds like a fancy phrase for looting."

If he doesn't like the looting idea, he really won't like my next suggestion, so I keep it to myself. *Or you can suffocate someone in a life-or-death scenario.*

———

I go for my run along the beach. I got lazy at Beechwood, let my training regime lapse. Dad was keen on us keeping fit and healthy to take on the physical demands of surviving – building shelters, chopping wood, whatever. Fighting off looters. We used to have a daily boot camp that left me sweating and exhausted.

I drop to the ground and do a set of press-ups and sit-ups. The wind whistles in from the North Sea and whips up the sand. There are a couple of dog walkers further down the beach, hurling balls into the shallows for the dogs to chase. My chest is tight. I breathe in slowly and close my eyes, letting myself feel battered by the wind, before I retreat to the calm of the path through the dunes, dodging dog poo and swirling rubbish as I run.

In the event of emergency, it's not a good idea to head for the coast – unless you're going for an evacuation by boat. Dad's voice is in my head, saying that I've cut off my options. One whole side of my location is inaccessible. *"What are you going to do when you're pinned down on one side, drown yourself? Stay one step ahead, Amber. That's the Rule."* Like a game of chess. If I move here, then what? Knight to F3. If my opponent moves there to counter, what should I do? Knight to F6. Anticipate, block, attack, defend. I've got out of the habit of thinking of the world like this. It's exhausting. But necessary.

The small café by the beach is tempting, all hazy glow and chatter through the steamed-up windows, but I need to save my cash until I know I've got access to more. I flick through a newspaper from the bin outside. Still no pictures of me. Maybe I'm just not Instagrammable enough. Good.

I think Josh is out when I get back, as the place is silent and in darkness. But when I push open the lounge door, I jump. He's sitting there, cross-legged on the floor, his fingertips touching in a Zen pose. One of Sue's scented candles is lit in front of him. He doesn't open his eyes.

"Is that you, Amber Warning?"

"Don't call me that. What are you doing?"

"Connecting. Thinking deep thoughts."

"Sure… Like, how long can I sponge off Amber?"

He rests a hand on his chest. "Now that hurts. Why do you feel the need to hit out at those who seek only to help you?"

"Stop! Stop the pseudo-yoga-guru voice."

"You might find meditation helps you too. Sit with me." He claps his hands together and then places them palm up on his knees. "Om," he chants.

"No way. Stop omming. It's weird."

He sighs and opens his eyes. He reaches across and touches my hand. "I get it, Amber. You and me, we've got major barriers up. Massive stonking protection barriers. Me because of my stepdad who used to beat the stuffing out of me. You – whatever you had going on with your family. But don't you get *tired* of living like that?"

"Have you taken something?" I ask. "Because when I left you earlier, you were looking for a needle to mend your jumper and now you're like full-on stage-three hippy."

"This helps me, OK. You might think it's rubbish; I did too at first. Sue got me into it to calm my brain down. I've been in some pretty dark places so if this helps me, I'm going to do it. It's up to you if you want to join in. Plus, what else are you going to do?"

I sit on the carpet beside him, copy his pose, listen to his voice as he tells me first to focus on the candle then to close my eyes and move through relaxing each part of my body. My mind wanders. I concentrate hard to pull it back. But I prefer a head full of busy noise to the alternative. Now he says we're off to find the thing we need. Someone in a woodland glade in our heads is going to pass us something.

"You're in the wood. You follow the path through the trees. Listen to the rustle of the leaves."

It's getting theatrical. He's enjoying having an audience. I half open an eye. He hasn't moved. I close my eyes again, shake out my arms, listen to his voice.

"Focus on the smell of the wood," he says. "The leaves, the mushrooms, the first shoots of new life pushing through the earth. Look at the trees, reaching up into the sky. Now follow them all the way back down, imagine the feel of the bark under your fingers, follow it back down to the roots, down, down into the earth."

I can't follow Josh's path through a carpet of snowdrops. My path is leading me to the woods I knew too well by our home in Wales. It's taking me to the iron gate. Dad's behind me.

All of a sudden my breathing is rapid, my palms sweating. *Stop*, I say in my head, then out loud. "JUST STOP IT."

I open my eyes, leap up and blow out the candle. The vanilla scent hits the back of my throat.

"Amber. What's the matter?" Josh looks concerned but I know he isn't. He can't be. He doesn't know me.

I slam the lounge door and retreat to the kitchen. I scrub

two baking potatoes and stab them before noisily shoving them into the microwave. I lay out the plates on the table, checking the straight lines of the cutlery. *Rule: Everything has its place.*

Josh joins me but says nothing. He opens a can of beans and scrapes it into a pan. He glances at me as he grates the last of the cheese.

"I just don't like walking in imaginary woods, OK," I blurt. "And I don't need anyone trying to help me. I manage by myself."

His mouth twitches into a half-smile and he opens it to say something but stops and shakes his head.

"What?" I snap back.

"Why do you think this place is always stocked with food? Why do you think Phil never changes the key code? I thought you were meant to be smart." He opens one of the cupboards and throws a packet of chicken Cup-a-Soup in my direction. "Phil and Sue don't eat all this processed stuff – and she's vegan. It's for us, Einstein. That's why they've never sold the place, why they hardly ever rent it out. They bring all their foster kids up here for a few days, let them know it's here. Phil and Sue, secret angels, keep it stocked with everything a drifter like me might need one day. A drifter like you. Food, clean sheets, plenty of toothpaste and shampoo."

He's right. I was too busy being cynical to see it. The Haven is Phil and Sue's version of an escape spot, for the kids like Josh or me who are too scared or too proud to ask when the shit hits.

There are good people too.

RULE:
ALWAYS HAVE YOUR GRAB-AND-GO BAG

Every prepper has their Grab-and-Go Bag. A Bug-out Bag or Go Bag that enables you to get through the first seventy-two hours of any emergency. You can debate endlessly about what exactly should be in the perfect Grab-and-Go Bag. A good night out for a prepper would be three hours of debate with another prepper about who has the best kit list. That's how we roll.

Some items are down to personal preference – I couldn't live without my tweezers and lip salve. Other items are standard, like hiking boots and waterproofs that could save your life. You can include a sentimental item like a photo or a toy. This one guy we used to know, with a couple of skull tattoos that peeped over his collar, seemed tough as anything to me but he kept a threadbare penguin at the bottom of his bag. I used to pester him to show me. It held way more appeal back then than first-aid kits or water purification tablets.

I liked it when others were there, in the early days. When Dad could still hold a rational conversation about prepping, when he could join in normal chats about last night's TV or the local rugby club. We had visitors; we went to barbecues. It wasn't all full-on survivalism.

But Dad changed over time. He hardened. He spent hours online or months away in the US doing 'research'. Soon he had no room for soft sentimental items. No room for sentiment. Your Grab-and-Go Bag stood between you and disaster. And he increasingly liked to dwell on disaster. What use was a cuddly penguin when looters were clearing the shops of food supplies? How could a soft toy save your life?

But when you're just a little kid, you'd rather have the penguin.

December

7

Today's door on the advent calendar reveals a tiny church with a tall steeple. God has made an appearance two days in a row. Anyone would think Christmas was something to do with Him, when everyone knows it's not any more. He must be fuming up there beyond the clouds, slowly blocked out of his own birthday celebrations.

Josh takes a while to get up. I'm still on school timetable but he's in permanent lounge lizard mode with no concept of time. He only moves when he wants to eat. He arrives rubbing his eyes, moving slowly.

I check through my Grab-and-Go Bag, adding a couple of instant food sachets I bought at the garage shop. Until this week, I'd not looked at it for ages. I'd gradually kicked the habit of laying out my kit each Sunday and ticking it off. Now, like an addict who's relapsed, I can't help myself repeatedly checking its contents.

"I need a few minutes online," I say. "What's it like for internet cafés up here?"

"You're joking, right?" Josh crunches through his toast. "If you want somewhere with an actual computer, not just Wi-Fi, there's nowhere like that round here. I use one at a church project sometimes, if I'm desperate. Don't you have a smartphone?"

"No. I don't want my dad to be able to use it to find me. Have you any idea how many apps use your data and your position?"

"All right, 007," he smirks. "The vicar at St Cuthbert's is probably the best bet then. Fancies himself as trendy. He's called Neville. I told him he's blown his chances of ever being made a bishop or a saint with that name. Saint Neville of Nowheresville. But as do-gooders go, he's not bad."

"First stop there, then. Hurry up." I take the jar of jam as he piles a spoonful on to another slice. He eats way too much sugar.

"I need the calories," he says. "Stop staring at me. I don't like people watching me eat."

I put the milk and butter back in the fridge and slam it shut. The glass jars in the door rattle.

"Relax, can't you," he says with a note of irritation in his voice. "No one's doing a room inspection. And stop laying the table like we're eighty. It's freaking me out."

Josh doesn't get it. He doesn't know the Rules.

"With any luck, there'll be a pile of donated food and stuff to take away at St Cuthbert's," he says. "We can pick up some bits and pieces."

"I bought us food," I say.

"You obviously didn't hear me. It's food and it's free. You can squirrel it away in your army bag. Stick with me. I'll show you the ropes. The right degree of grateful. The right degree of truth to share and lies to tell." He wipes his toast round the plate to scoop up the blobs of jam he's missed. His mouth full, he adds, "It's a minefield out there but I'm pretty good at all this crap now."

We head for the bus stop before Josh decides we should cut across the fields instead. "Never waste a bus fare if you don't mind walking. Learn from the master."

He strides off down the road before taking a stile and a signed footpath. "On the Josh homeless youth tour. Follow me." He prats about, leading the way with his arm raised above him like a tour guide. "On the left, a stinky pond. And on the right, we have a cowpat, ladies and gentlemen. Typical for the area. Keep up, please, missy at the back."

He suddenly stops and puts his finger to his lips. He whispers, "A heron!" and points towards the water. I catch the glint of a fish disappearing down the bird's throat, which expands to take it.

"It's a good omen," he says.

"Of what? What's it mean?"

"Restless loner, a heron. Like me. Come on." He runs across the grass, pulling me with him, full into the wind, blowing back my hair and sucking out my breath. We stop at last, panting on the crest of the hill, and the dunes and sea stretch out beneath us.

"My gran would have called this 'blowing away the cobwebs'," he says into the wind. His words are sad and lost on the breeze. It's the first time he's mentioned anyone in his family fondly. But he uses the past tense. "You can breathe out here. People leave you alone." He retreats into the fake-fur-lined hood on his parka.

The clouds are scudding across the sky in the wind. I close my eyes and feel the cold air on my face.

RULE:
I AM THE RULES AND
THE RULES ARE ME

Dad lay sprawled across the sofa, a collection of beer cans at his feet. The room smelled bad – of sweat and stale beer. Relief mixed with revulsion. He was dead to the world, meaning I could be myself for a few brief hours before he woke up.

I liked him being fast asleep. I could pad around the house, unobserved, poking into things I wasn't meant to see.

I could be me again for a while.

I looked at the wall and my heart missed a beat. There was a new Rule scrawled at the top with the ink smudged, the writing erratic. Like it had been written by a madman – which effectively it had. What was the point in pretending otherwise any more?

I AM THE RULES AND THE RULES ARE ME.

Childlike in its horrid simplicity. That basically summed up the whole wall. What Dad said went.

However stupid.

However loopy.

However damaging.

I tiptoed past him and stood outside in the rain, letting it soak into my hair and run down my cheeks. I looked up at the sky through blurry, misty eyes and sought the reassurance of a distant star. I wanted a sense of the size of the universe, to reduce the significance of my tiny corner of it. I thought that my problems would shrink if I saw I was just a small dot standing in a garden in Wales in the UK in the northern hemisphere. But it was too cloudy to see any glimmer of stars.

And all I felt was cold and shivery and hopeless.

December

7

By the time Josh and I get across the many fields and scrape the mud off our shoes on the tarmac, there's already a motley-looking crowd assembled outside St Cuthbert's. A guy with a dog is arguing with a middle-aged lady in a lilac cardigan about whether the dog can go in. It strains at the end of its leash, teeth bared. I hope she says no.

"I know the back way," says Josh, steering me round the corner and through the disabled-access door, which opens wide to reveal the makeshift café in the church hall beyond. Bacon sandwiches and carrot soup are being served at a long communal table. At the far side, there's a desk headed 'Here to Help station' where a vicar is tapping away at a keyboard.

He leaps up when he sees Josh and shakes his hand vigorously. "Josh, good to see you back. Looking well. Read those John Wyndham books yet? Who's this?"

"This is Scarlet, a friend of mine. Can we go online for a bit, Vicar?"

I raise an eyebrow at him – Scarlet?

"Good to meet a friend of Josh's," says the vicar, shaking my hand too and beaming. "Fancy some hot food, Scarlet?"

I know it's ungrateful of me, that these types have a vocation or whatever, that they mean well. But I instinctively don't like him. It's not his fault. I just don't like that this stranger in a black shirt and dog collar is doing something to help me. I don't like needing help. I grunt a reply while he clears a space on the table and picks through leaflets to hand us.

"Play nice, Scarlet," whispers Josh.

I grit my teeth and take his leaflets on not sharing needles and nod sagely at them. I just need his computer not his life advice. At last he's called away to deal with angry-dog-man out front and we sit down.

"Why did you pick Scarlet? What's next, Colonel Mustard?"

"Traffic lights. Red, amber, green. Scarlet seemed the natural choice. I'll go for green next time. Jade?" He laughs. "Or maybe Olive. Olive, definitely. Going to tell me what you're looking for?" He's using the corner of a leaflet on STDs to hook out the dirt from under his fingernails.

"I want to see what my dad is up to. To see where he is. That's all."

I take a deep breath. Until this week, I've been shutting him out, pretending he didn't exist. That what happened to me, to him, was all a terrible dark fairy tale. I haven't wanted to search him out, to see how he's doing, or where he ended up. A defence mechanism to pretend that something hasn't happened.

"The real bastards mess with your head wherever they are." Josh squeezes my shoulder. "When was the last time you saw him?"

"Over two years ago," I say quietly. "I wasn't planning on ever having to see him again."

I wait for Josh to start talking to someone else and then I begin checking forums on prepping and survivalism. I feel clammy and sick when I find the first picture of Dad – Ellis Fitzpatrick resurrected. He's posted plenty in the last couple of months, sharing his muddled thoughts. Looks like he's embraced social media again after his previous paranoia about surveillance. His posts have many likes, many comments.

I scroll through blogs on possible bug-out places, the merits of off-the-peg bunkers over buried shipping containers or disused missile silos. He runs through the advantages of taking over existing buildings versus rural bug-out places that can be self-sufficient. I click on an article about fortification which praises a prison as the best place to live after the SHTF. It's coherent, well argued. I can't believe he wrote it. I assume he cut and pasted it from someone else.

Yes, seems like my dad has been a busy little prepper. Snapshots of kit, of artistic interpretations of some of the Rules. Putting something in a curly font doesn't make it intrinsically nicer. He hasn't laid out all the Rules – even he must see that would be extreme. He's picked the ones like *Leave no trace* that sound more sensible, greener – as though he's thinking about the planet rather than himself. It seems to be working. For him.

Dad's shared his wisdom on bushcraft, foraging and survival skills. I enlarge a photo of him – he's older but he looks surprisingly well; tanned and healthy. I study it for some clue to what he's really like now. But our family was always good at putting on a mask.

Josh startles me by leaning over my shoulder and angles the screen towards him to have a better look. "You're so like him," he says. "Minus the stubble and the Adam's apple."

"I'm nothing like him." *Being* like him, ending up anything like him, scares me. Blood is thicker than water. I can't escape it.

"Jeez, you weren't joking," he says, scrolling down the screen. "He really is preparing for Armageddon. Cool."

Not cool.

"There are closed groups," I say. "I need to log in as me to access them. If I do, am I traceable?"

Josh shrugs. "Do I look like I'd know? Even if he could trace it, it gets him to the vicar's laptop in St Cuthbert's."

My fingers hesitate, hovering above the keys. I log in. I go straight to the closed survivalist groups I know he set up. And there he is – repeat posting about me. Asking for help looking for me, his beloved daughter, Amber; flashing an out-of-date picture. Me in a pair of denim dungarees, in the woods, his arm loosely round my shoulders in a gesture that looks like affection or pride but wasn't. Like the game Happy Families. Mr Fitzpatrick the Prepper. Miss Fitzpatrick the Prepper's daughter. As though we're living some off-grid dream. What the snapshot *doesn't* show is the moments before Mum took the photo and the moments after it. It doesn't show her broken collarbone and black eye because she did something wrong when taking it. Mrs Fitzpatrick the Prepper's unhappy wife.

I click through to Events. Dad smiles out of the screen with a big timbered hall behind him. The post is from Devon a few days ago. A shiver runs through me. He's here. In the UK. Not Florida. I was right to leave Beechwood.

And I can't go back.

He's giving talks called 'Prepping: Sustainable ways of living in the future'. One's near a place we went camping when I was about ten – after he'd come back from another long stay in the States. He'd fixed up a rope swing and I jumped in the river again and again until dusk. He wrapped me in a towel and blanket and cooked our supper on a campfire while we watched for kingfishers in the half-light. I loved it – the freedom of it.

Looks like he's on a month's tour up and down the country, building on interest in sustainable living and fears about the future. People are buying tickets to see him speak. You can't cut and paste a talk like he did with the articles, can't blag it. He really must have got his act together, laying on the charm that he saves for other people. No one would believe me over him.

I copy the dates and places on to the edge of one of the leaflets. At least I'll know exactly where Dad is – maybe it'll all be over after the talks. I let a tiny glimmer of hope take hold. Perhaps he'll go back to the US.

"We could go along to one if you like," says Josh. "Maybe he's changed. He looks pretty normal. Could be worth seeing what he's saying."

"How much can people *really* change?" I say. "He'll be pushing the same doom or SHTF scenarios he always did, just in a smarter outfit."

I minimize Dad with a click of the mouse.

About the time I started secondary school, we began to live our life in a heightened state of alert. Dad pored over newspapers and we always had the low hum of a radio on in case war was declared when we weren't paying attention. All that dwelling on doomsday takes a toll on your state of well-being.

I have a counsellor, Dr Meadows, lined up by Julie, who talks me though stuff about Mum. Mostly I sit there, saying nothing, playing through the Rules in my mind or calculating the area of the carpet tiles. But that psychology stuff can get in your head even if you don't want it to. It pops up in the middle of the night and makes you think about it, even if you squeeze your eyes shut and put on your headphones. Makes you think about what's normal and not normal. About what you can move on from and what you can't ever leave behind.

Has Dad changed? Can anyone shed what they were, what they did? Or is it always there, underneath the surface? Waiting for the pretence to crack.

RULE:
EVERYTHING HAS ITS PLACE

There was a preppers' collective with a private Facebook group and occasional meet-ups. They figured that by pooling expertise and buying-power, they could act in the common good. One guy worked at a wholesaler and used his staff discount for buying pallets of goods to be shared out. Dad had always been obsessive about using any BOGOF offers for stockpiling. One packet of rice for us, one for the store. But this way, they could scale it up and get a better discount. Our food store grew bigger and bigger. It started in the cupboard under the stairs but as it expanded it was split between the attic and the spare bedroom. Once we moved to the farm, we had a whole outbuilding. I spent hours with Dad cataloguing toilet paper and food supplies. We arranged cans in strict date order, using up any food as it neared use-by dates, restocking and rotating the shelves.

Like everything, he had a system that he agonized over and which became crazier over time.

Rule: Everything has its place. Cans and jars should face forwards and be exactly one centimetre apart.

I had to use a ruler – a wooden one that hurt when Dad rapped it across my knuckles if I got it wrong. Soon, I could tell by eye alone.

But the collective grew into more than discussing the price of canned tomatoes. The meetings grew longer. They acted like a war cabinet preparing for a conflict that might never come – but they secretly wished it would.

Dad had a magnetism about him at times. A strange charm. A loser who'd dropped out of college, out of any job he'd ever had, in and out of his relationship with Mum, his own parents, and fatherhood most of the time; suddenly, with the collective, he had people looking up to him. That must have been a whole new experience. The preppers in Wales wanted to know what Dad had to say. What the latest ideas were.

He'd talk about a state-of-the-art bunker complex down in Arizona, or a nature-loving survivalist community in Alaska. He wheedled his way into a Facebook group of part-time preppers who held high-paid jobs in Silicon Valley. They wanted a little insurance-policy real estate in the wilds somewhere for when their own IT creations brought about the AI singularity and the collapse of human civilisation. That's irony for you.

He'd brag about his contacts at those meetings:

"Jeez, when I was with the folks out in Mill Falls, they were experimenting with…"

"I was discussing water filtration last week with Kurt in Portland…"

"The advice I gave to the group in Boston…"

Looking back, I don't know how much of what Dad said was true. Did these communities he talked about even exist? If they did, had he ever been more than a casual visitor? He came to bill himself as an expert. And if all those places were so amazing, why wasn't he living in any of them, instead of here, with us?

Social media lets people like my dad exist in a bubble of mutual appreciation. And however extreme one person is, there's always someone else who takes things just that little bit further. A guy in the desert in Nevada with a store of hand grenades to take out the Feds loved my dad. And an army veteran with a long grey beard and tattooed face who hated everyone and everything, really connected with him.

Maybe all the wise and normal preppers were just too busy holding down average jobs to come into our orbit, too busy digging potatoes at their allotments or maintaining a sensible cardboard box of supplies in the garage. We used to know people like that but they dropped away as Dad got more extreme and wore a camo waistcoat. But there were others who still wanted to listen to him, to hang on his every word. He was only too happy to oblige on those evenings back in Wales, telling people how it should be done.

"We have turned our backs on looking after our families properly ourselves." This was the start of one of his regular trains of thought. Mum bowed her head and picked at the patterned flowers on her skirt. I sat up stiffly beside her.

We were Exhibit A. Again. We were evidence that Dad had a family he looked after. Mum put crisps in bowls as her attempt at being a hostess. She wore a cardigan so no one could see the bruises on her arm.

"It is our responsibility to rebuild when all this modern world fails, when modern medicine fails, when the international systems fail."

Disaster after disaster. Just like my Show and Tell.

"It may well not be the virus that gets any of us, it's the *person* carrying the virus. It's the person fleeing the virus, right? We all know them – the person who hasn't seen fit to prepare for their family, as we have done."

Pause for self-congratulatory murmurings.

"Normal rules, normal law and order will disappear. Your gentle old neighbour who wouldn't hurt a fly will no longer have the threat of police and the justice system standing between him and looting your home. And as for those who already have criminal records – or the prisoners released from the broken prisons – they'll be rushing to fill the anarchic gap."

He lets this sink in. People look around, wondering

which of them is the threat, which of them is the bad guy. (*Spoiler alert* It's Dad).

"We're gonna need to gather together, like the old wagon trains in the Wild West, able to defend ourselves." He picked up his glass of water and drank it slowly, the sound of his swallowing loud in the hushed room.

"We should all be prepared to fight for our lives in the chaos that will descend. 'Kill or be killed'."

Pause for dramatic effect.

"We have a right to defend ourselves and our families," he said, looking around the table, making eye contact with each and every member of the group. "An inalienable right to bear arms back where I'm from. How in this little country of yours do we get ourselves some weapons?"

How did he get from canned tomatoes to wanting a shotgun?

Easy. This is how it worked with the Rules: Dad would start off with something that sounded reasonable, sensible. For example, take the Rule: *Everything has its place*. A sensible way to live. No time wasted looking for anything because everything is where it should be. Keys in the dish by the door, plasters in the first-aid cabinet. Everything where it should be when you need it. Sensible.

But then as he got worse he added sub-clauses. First, it was about the food storage:

Cans and jars should face forwards and be exactly one centimetre apart. Then it was the place settings. There was a whole unnecessary rule with a diagram of how knives and forks and spoons had to be arranged on the table, like we were working at Downton Abbey rather than having some beans on toast on a second-hand IKEA table. And then it moved into how our clothes should be arranged so that if the SHTF inconsiderately in the middle of the night, boy, were we ready. Other people would be turning their jeans out the right way round and looking for clean underwear but for us: *Sets of clothes should be laid out in order, ready to put on in an emergency. Working left to right: underwear, trousers, top, warmer top, socks then shoes.*

Mum had to lay his clothes out too, while she was still around, and then it was my job. Because *Everything has its place* turned out to apply to us too, in an unspoken way. Mum's place became tending the vegetable patch, cooking his meals, sitting beside him like a quiet mouse or walking three paces behind him.

And Dad's place?

WHEREVER HE DAMN WELL WANTED.

```
┌─────────────┐
│ December    │
├─────────────┤
│    7        │
│          ◁  │
└─────────────┘
```

I close the vicar's laptop.

"Come on, fancy a free bacon butty?" says Josh, nudging my shoulder.

We queue up as Josh lectures me about why he never goes online. I'm beginning to understand why he's lacking friends.

"You're in an even worse mood than usual, I can sense these things," he says. "Screens and social media make everyone feel bad about themselves. The more we get connected, the more disconnected we really are." He hands me a stewed cup of tea and a bacon sandwich. I pull off the white strip of fat and scrape the thick butter from the bread. "That's why I had to quit social media totally," he says. "The monetization of our distraction – I read it somewhere."

"Online probably," I say.

"Hilarious. I couldn't leave it alone – like, I was 'on' twenty-four-seven. Gran said I'm wired differently from other people."

"You'd make a good prepper," I say. "Preppers don't like dependence on modern tech that can fail in a matter of hours. Other skills are way more important than being able to google."

Neville's hovering to the side, glancing in our direction. "I think the Rev wants to try saving me again," whispers Josh through the last of his bread roll. "And you're fresh blood, so don't think you're going to get out of here without the lecture either. That's the price. Everything has a price. The vicar's one is better than lots of others I've been asked to pay." He slurps down the tea. "A good-looking boy like me has to watch his back, if you know what I mean."

"Not Neville?" I say.

"No, not him. But you never know. Never let your guard down, Scarlet Woman. Don't drink. Don't take drugs. Never ever be alone with these people."

For all his breezy, cheery nature, Josh has developed his own set of rules. Survival rules. Rules to stop himself being robbed, being abused. *Trust no one.*

"Luckily I've developed an amazing BS detector," he says, opening and closing his fist on top of his head as he makes a siren noise. "I have a sixth sense for when someone's trying to put one over on me."

I notice the time on the big clock on the wall. Right about now, I'd be back in my room at Beechwood, thinking about what's for dinner and how much homework I've got. Instead I'm taking lessons from Josh in how to keep myself safe.

Josh pokes my arm. "Why don't you post something in those groups along the lines of: Don't worry, everything's fine. Don't look for me. I want to be alone for a while because my dad's a psycho, et cetera, et cetera." He picks at the food stuck in his front teeth.

"It's not that easy. My social worker, all the team behind her – they're pleased to have found Dad. He's a manipulator, a control freak. I've got no chance against what he'd say." I pull my coat tighter. Even in the warmth and bustle of this church hall and with a full stomach and surrounded by well-meaning people, Dad can reach me.

Josh mutters something I can't make out.

"What?" I say, pulling at his arm.

"Nothing. It's just that it seems to me you're letting your dad have a fine old time swanning around wherever he likes while you, well, *hide*. I thought you were more kickass than that. That's all. Coming to check out the freebies?"

Josh is right. I'm letting Dad win. But how can I possibly end this once and for all when he holds all the cards?

———

Josh cons the vicar into giving us a lift back by telling a vile story about a sore on his calf and offering to roll up his trousers. He says it's too bad to carry back all these cans from the food bank. The vicar looks sad. I think he knows Josh is lying about the bad leg. When he puts Josh's coat in the boot, loose change falls from the pockets. Change he didn't have when we went in there – money he obviously stole from the now-empty donations plate by the door. The vicar says nothing. He picks up the scattered coins and hands them back to Josh. Maybe we're a test of his faith. It would be too easy to be kind to good people. I sit on the back seat of his clapped-out Ford Fiesta hugging my plastic bag of free stuff, blocking out his mini-sermon that Jesus loves everybody no matter what they do.

So that the vicar doesn't find out exactly where we're staying, I get him to drop us in the village rather than right by The Haven. He's in a rush for a service.

"God bless," he says, with a note of sadness, and the car accelerates slowly away.

"A very successful trip," says Josh, holding up his bag. "Internet, lunch, tea. Free stuff. You can have my sanitary products if I can have your mushroom soup."

"You didn't have to steal the money," I say.

"If they leave loose change lying around, someone is going to take it. May as well be us. Some of those other guys would transform it straight into a can of Special Brew." He sets off down the street. I'm still cross with him. Why should it matter to me if he's stealing a few quid from that vicar's church?

But it does matter. It draws attention. It creates risk.

The ginger-haired guy from the shop slows alongside us on his bike, his brakes squeaking. "All right?" he says. Josh nods in greeting. He looks at our bags. "Hope you've not been shopping with the opposition."

Josh laughs. "Course not. No money was exchanged, was it, Amber?"

I shrink into my coat.

"See you around, Josh. Amber." He looks me in the eyes, and I know he's working out I was lying about my nan owning a cottage. He cycles off, glancing back at us.

Josh, the friendly idiot who can't keep his mouth shut, has told him my name.

I don't join in Josh's hippy meditation tonight. He closes the lounge door and I do my own thinking in the kitchen. Josh will realize I haven't quite told the truth about how I left Beechwood if I tell him I'm off because he let slip my name. Or he'll think that I'm a paranoid weirdo. Or both. But I didn't like the way the guy from the shop was looking at me. He's now made a connection between Josh, The Haven and me. And he knows my first name. What if there's something in the news tomorrow or the next day? Dad used to say that we should rely on our survival instinct. We're animals like any other. I should trust my instincts. I've stayed in one spot for too long. It's too risky.

I stretch my map across the table. I need to get away from here. Back inland. Somewhere that's not full of CCTV and police, where me and a rucksack can go unremarked. I scan through the place names, look at areas of countryside and footpaths. Hadrian's Wall, maybe. I realize I'm not too far from a prepping community that Dad linked up with to share info on emergency resources. We came up to visit them years ago. The idea was that our group could use their bug-out house if our own was blocked by floods, aliens, hungry mobs, etc. We would do the same for them in return. It could be useful now to access an empty bug-out property – if I could find it.

I look at the place names, waiting for something to spark a memory. Mum and I didn't go to the house but I know it'll be somewhere off the beaten track.

Josh surfaces, wafting a sickly aroma of joss sticks. "Changed your mind yet about going to see one of your dad's shows?"

"First, it's not a show. He's not a magician. Second, what don't you understand about trying to *avoid* someone?"

"Aren't you a tiny bit curious?"

"No. I know exactly what he's like. Isn't there a saying about putting lipstick on a pig? He's still a pig. I'm not going near him or his talks."

"Whatever. Message received." He flips the map to see what I'm looking at. "If you want to travel over to Hadrian's Wall, I know all the dodges. Best doorways, bus shelters en

route. A few mates scattered about where I can sofa surf."
He beams and whispers, "I could make sure you never have
to resort to the poo shovel."

"I'm fine, thanks." I fold the map and pack it in the top
flap of my rucksack.

"Or if you've got cash, there are B&Bs, pubs – all geared
up to people walking the wall. *Have* you got any cash?" He
looks directly at me but I say nothing. There's no way I'm
telling him about the rolled-up notes I sleep with in my
pillowcase. Not after the donations plate. *Trust no one.*

"I could be your muscle," he adds, flexing his scrawny
biceps.

"That would require you to have more muscle than me
in the first place."

"Ouch. Maybe not the muscle, but safety in numbers?
Witty repartee? Encyclopedic knowledge of bus routes?"
He fiddles around with the magnetic letters on the fridge
door. "Spooky – if I add an L to the letters in your name, it
spells Ramble. See. We have to go walking together – it's
written in ye olde runes."

I chew my lip. Could I bear to have him along? Or should
I stomach it because a couple travelling makes more sense
than a teenager on her own in December?

He isn't giving up. "Hang on. There's something perfect
I fished out of a bin in Carlisle a while back." He pulls a
faded T-shirt from the radiator. It's printed with a Roman
helmet and the slogan 'I walked the wall'. Josh is beaming

at me. "I've *literally* got the T-shirt! You've got to take me now."

"All right. But don't make me regret it. And it's a short-term thing."

He sorts through the drying clothes, humming. "When are we going? I need to get my pants dry but they're not far off."

"After breakfast in the morning."

"Righto, Sergeant Major." Josh reaches on top of the fridge and gropes for something. "This calls for a little celebration. Do me a favour – Phil keeps a stash of wine in the shed, locked away from any little kiddywinkies." He throws me the key he's retrieved. "I have something else to finish off while you're out of the way."

"Like what?" Does he want to snoop through my things?

"Something nice. Don't panic, Ms Paranoid."

I pick up the rubber torch hanging by the back door and go to the end of the garden, picking my way across the slippery crazy paving. The moon disappears behind a cloud. I unlock the door. I hesitate. It's the smell that triggers something. The staleness, the damp.

The shed is dark and small and as I force myself to step inside the torch flickers. I tap it against my leg and it brightens again, shining dimly on a couple of deckchairs. My heart's speeding up. I ignore it. The door bangs in the wind. The box marked 'Phil's stuff' is on the shelf by the beach things. I carefully lay down the torch to point inside while I select a bottle of Prosecco. The torch flickers out. Panicking, I grab at it, knocking the plastic buckets and spades off the shelf with a clatter. I can't get the light back on. I fumble with the battery compartment, releasing the batteries, and rub them together in my hands to warm them up but I'm shaking so much that one drops to the ground. I grope around for it by my feet and when I've found it I count slowly through the Rules, trying to suppress the panic. They're painted on the walls, they're in my head. They're always in my head. Dad screaming them at me, demanding I recite them back to him.

Rule: Trust no one. Rule: Always have your Grab-and-Go Bag.

Though it's cold out here, I'm boiling hot, sweat patches forming under my arms. *Rule: Survival is everything.*

I reinsert the batteries, my shaking hands struggling to close the plastic flap.

Rule: Honour thy father. Rule: Never break the Rules.

I'm dizzy. If I don't get out of here I'm going to keel over. But the light flickers back on. I'm in a shed with punctured beach balls and a windbreak. Josh is calling me from the kitchen door. I wait until my breath stabilizes, counting in for five and out for five. I take the bottle and return to being a normal person. Almost.

Back in the kitchen, I pour us two glasses with shaking hands and gulp at the wine. Josh is so hyped up he doesn't notice anything.

"I brought you a gift," he says, his cheeks rosy with the cold. Bits of greenery are caught in his hair. "As it's our last evening before we hit the road." He pulls me into the lounge, his hands over my eyes. "I give you – Josh's grotty Christmas grotto. Ta-dah!"

Sprigs of holly hang over the pictures and lengths of ivy are stretched across the fireplace, woven round the advent calendar, and hanging down loosely at the sides. Two long socks dangle from the mantelpiece, held in place by Sue's hideous ornaments. The semi-dead fir tree from the front garden is propped up in a bucket, topped by a cardboard star cut from a cereal packet. All Sue's candles are lit, the twinkling flames reflected in the mirror and casting shadows around the room.

He's made something beautiful from nothing at all. I want to tell him, but the words catch in my throat. Instead, I reach out and take his hand and squeeze it.

Rule:
Honour thy father

He took that one from the Ten Commandments, the edited version. The real one, the original, was *Honour thy father and mother*. But he purged my mother from history. As far as he was concerned, there was only one person who should get the honouring: him.

'Thy' and 'honour' – old-fashioned words that he used to make his Rules seem more powerful. As though me honouring him was written down thousands of years ago, etched in stone tablets, inscribed in hieroglyphs on a pyramid somewhere. Rather than the reality of shouty big letters on a wall in a rundown farm in a remote part of Wales. But why not? Dad was the supreme emperor of all he surveyed. He was Darth Sidious or Julius Caesar sitting in the arena and watching all I did; he was the one with the power to control how my day went merely by raising his thumb up or down. The power to control how my whole *life* was going to pan out.

But even empires must fall one day.

I'm up before Josh, checking my kit. I pick up the advent calendar from the mantelpiece. I've been away a week. Julie could've been suspended or sacked because of me. I hope she's OK because, let's face it, no one else would give her a job. Today's door reveals a Christmas tree, covered in gaudy baubles. They've been popping up in windows in the village, flashing brightly coloured lights. I prefer the Christmas scene Josh created last night, which I now carefully dismantle, restoring the room to soullessness.

As we lock up The Haven, all traces of my stay erased, I place my set of keys back in the key box and give the squat little house one last, long look. I can't come back here. Josh and his big mouth has put paid to that.

We walk through the village and sit on the wall by the bus stop. It's strange to be back on the road again not knowing exactly where we'll be tomorrow.

"Might snow tonight," says Josh, sniffing at the air. "Fear not. I'm weighing up the options. It's between a bijou squat I know or a backpackers' place where we can stay in exchange for cleaning duties. Off the record, like."

I point to my rucksack. "We'd fit right in at a backpackers'. People coming and going. And it'll be quiet this time of year too. Perfect." I put on my beanie hat and gloves. He might be right about the snow. I wrap my massive scarf across my face as we get on the bus and make a beeline for the back seat. Josh is a complete bus nerd. He chatters on about how they're warm, dry, something different to see out of the window, usually no hassle.

"Mostly it's just something to do," he says. "Like the London cabbies with the Knowledge, I'm hot on the bus routes, the fares, the best seats, which ones have charging points. Yeah, baby. I'm your man."

Most people would make fun of him for it, but Dad would have rated Josh's useful life knowledge. And it makes me feel better about letting him stick around for a few days, big mouth or not.

I'm feeling travel sick on Josh's beloved bus by the time it reaches the bus station where we need to change. I'm glad of a break in the fresh air though Josh does his best to ruin it with a greasy, smelly burger.

We're the only people getting the next bus and the driver is in no rush to start off, wanting to talk about the weather.

I just want to sit down out of sight.

"Going walking?" he asks.

"Yep. We're mad keen walkers," says Josh. "She's got a map and a compass."

"Feel the cold, do you?" the driver calls out to me. "Picked the wrong day to go hiking."

"She's got a thing about scarves," replies Josh as he walks back through the bus towards me. "They're her comfort blanket. Soft and cuddly." He sits right up next to me. "Yep, soft and cuddly, just like you!" He prods my arm. "Bet no one has ever called you that before!"

"Why do you have to chat to everyone? Can't we just get on a bus without giving away our life story?" I fold my arms and shrink into the seat by the window.

Josh manages a whole three minutes without speaking. But he can't stop himself. He *is* wired differently, like his gran said. He pulls out a paperback and taps me with it. "The vicar lent it me. John Wyndham. I'm reading all of his now. This one – you'd like it – everyone, nearly everyone, is blind after this big meteor shower and then if that wasn't bad enough giant man-killer plants are on the rampage. The main characters head for the country like you're planning. But I'm thinking it's not going to end well. Plants *like* the countryside."

"Killer plants weren't on the SHTF list."

"It *is* hard to take seriously as a threat. Think giant Venus flytrap. Maybe it was scarier in the fifties. It was probably on TV – those little black and white ones with the aerial on top. But, and this is where America has the edge in all those disaster or dystopia movies, they've always got the Statue of Liberty or the New York library or some massive skyscraper to hang out in. This one's in Wiltshire! Name me an interesting big thing in Wiltshire."

"Stonehenge. That's in Wiltshire."

"Just big rocks in a circle – not a building to hide in, is it. They'd never shoot a blockbuster there."

I close my eyes and let him witter on. Just for a while it feels normal. Like I'm back at Beechwood, lounging around the common room, listening to the others talking about movies I haven't seen, trying to pretend I belong there.

———

I must have nodded off with the motion of the bus because I wake up to find Josh shaking me. "Stop dribbling and snoring. We're nearly at the backpackers' place."

We've gained a couple of elderly passengers while I've been asleep but neither of them is getting off at our stop. I scramble to pull up my scarf but it slips as I manhandle my huge bag down the aisle.

"Enjoy your walking," calls the driver and pulls away, giving us a cheery wave.

I shouldn't have let him see my face like that. And we could have flown across Europe in the time it's taken us to do this journey from The Haven.

The backpackers' hostel is a large, stone Victorian building set back from the road in a flat landscape. Not pretty, but solid and reliable. Too large to be a private house, way too ordinary to be a stately home. A minibus of French teenagers is unloading noisily by the front door. I thought it would be less busy than this in December.

"Stick with me, Olive," says Josh with a wink. He pushes past the French group with a loud '*Excusez-moi, mes enfants*' delivered in a broad Yorkshire accent, pulling me through by the hand.

"All right, Kev!" he says and high-fives the harassed-looking man on reception. "Need some help for a few nights? Brought my cousin, Olive." Josh leans in and whispers loudly, "She's no trouble, very quiet. Completely mute after a terrible incident with a trumpet. Just one of those tragic accidents."

"Still spouting nonsense, I see," says Kev. He pushes a key across the counter. "You can have room 11. Report back in half an hour and I'll have some jobs for you."

I don't know whether I'm pretending to be mute or not, so I just nod and smile stiffly at him and follow Josh.

"What was all that about? Mute?"

He smirks at me. "I thought I'd have a break from you telling me off – though not sure Kev quite believed the trumpet story."

"I don't tell you off."

"You do. *And* you have a killer death stare. Giving me

daggers over too much jam on my toast."

"We do three nights only and move on," I say. "I don't want to stay anywhere too long."

"Promise. Though you're going to love it so much you'll be begging me to stay."

He unlocks the door to room 11. It's a family room with a double bed and bunk bed, uncomfortable chairs and table and an en-suite bathroom with a grubby shower curtain. The only decoration is a faded print of a Roman soldier hanging above the bed and a dusty vase of dried flowers on the windowsill.

Josh stretches out across the double bed, kicking off his shoes, and tests the springiness.

"I don't like bunk beds," I say flatly.

He flips his lower lip with his finger and says, "Diddums!" and shows no sign of moving.

I unpack my clothes and arrange them in the correct piles, socks ready in shoes. I don't sit on the bunk bed. I pointedly sit on the chair until Josh 'unpacks'. He opens a drawer and tips in the contents of his bag. I hold myself back from tidying it or saying anything. *Everything has its place.* I know it's weird to other people. I push in his drawer, so I don't have to look at it as we leave to report to Kev. He wants us to spend an hour cleaning straight away.

The 'mute Olive' routine from Josh is wearing thin. It wasn't funny in the first place, but he doesn't know when to stop with it. Josh doesn't have a filter, doesn't pick up when he's being annoying. I leave him in the corridor mopping floors while I go back to the cupboard for the glass cleaner. As I reach for it off the top shelf, the door swings shut behind me. There's no handle on the inside. Now I can see the paper sign on the back of the door saying '*Caution – keep the door wedged open while using this cupboard*'. It's like a nonsense rule from *Alice in Wonderland* as I can only read it when it's too late. I pull at the woodwork and doorframe, before the panic takes hold. There's no gap to prise open.

I knock loudly. Josh will come. It won't be long before he'll miss me. Surely?

"Hey! I can't open the door. Hello!"

It's just a cupboard. The same cupboard it was before the door shut. The light's on. I'll be out in a minute, tops. Everything is fine.

I try to breathe deeply. I lean back on the door and scan the space. About twelve cubic metres. No window. I close my eyes. In my head I'm back *there*. Locked in, with the complete darkness and the stale air. The scuttling rats.

I count through the Rules again, like I did then. Like I always do. My mantra, my creed.

Rule: Prep for the worst.

Rule: The only useful knowledge is the stuff that keeps you alive.

I bang on the door and shout. This time it's more frenzied.

Rule: Use your weakness as your strength.

Rule: Honour thy father.

I take the mop and metal bucket and bash them together like a clanging drum.

Rule: Stay one step ahead.

The minutes are ticking by. This is how it starts, measured in minutes then hours then days.

I can't breathe. I pull at my top to relieve the pressure of something pushing on my chest. I'm going to die. My hands are going numb. I stretch out my fingers and lean against the wall.

"Open this damn door!" I shout.

The door opens and Kev's there, frowning. I swear he looks at the back of the door for damage rather than checking I'm OK.

"Why the hell haven't you got a proper door on this cupboard? Have you heard of a handle? Of health and safety?" I explode in a red-faced torrent.

Josh is powering up the corridor. "It's a miracle!" he says. "She can speak again! I've got this, mate." He enfolds me in a hug. I'm sure he wants to stop me from taking a swipe at Kev. He pats my back. "Olive, the new trauma has replaced the old trauma. You can speak once more."

More nonsense from Josh and a promise to tidy up has Kev shuffling back to reception.

"That was truly hilarious," says Josh, ignoring the fact that I'm shaky and pale. "Did you see Kev's face?"

I feel faint. The adrenaline has drained away. I sit down.

"Amber? You're OK, yeah?"

I nod but say nothing. I don't want him to know how a stupid cupboard full of mops and buckets can reduce me to this.

"Just claustrophobic," I say, still not moving. Josh tidies away our stuff and pulls me up.

"We need to get out of here for a bit before you lock yourself in any more small spaces. Come on, we'll see the local attraction before it shuts – it's why there's a hostel here in the first place. Some Roman ruins.

"I'm not in the mood for…"

"What? Enjoying yourself? Unwinding? Learning something? I bet your dad isn't spending every waking minute thinking about you. Why do him the honour of having him on the brain all the time? Get something else to think about. It works for me."

He has a point. But it isn't that easy. I can't get those photos of Dad out of my head.

"We can dress up as centurions and you can hit me with replica weapons," adds Josh. "That'll cheer you up."

"Centurion House! That's the name I've been trying to remember. Of a bug-out place up here. Dad said it had the starriest skies he'd ever seen because it was near an observatory in the national park. I couldn't remember the name until you said that."

"See. Aren't you glad you brought me along?"

Rule:
The only useful knowledge is the stuff that keeps you alive

Dad threw my history folder across the table, scattering its contents. I stopped myself from picking it up, clasping my hands tight behind my back.

That was how the fear got you. What was the right thing to do? What would get the least reaction from him? You become unsure of yourself. Of your own responses.

You, the essence of you, learns to back off, to fade away, into what *he* wants to see.

Mum had got good at it. So good she became a shadow before my eyes.

I didn't want to become a shadow.

Option 1: Pick up the folder, clear up the mess.
Option 2: Ignore it. Do not argue that the essay was important. Agree he was right to treat it as he did.

Because, somehow, in Dad's world, my getting educated was an affront to all he stood for. Because *he* knew everything we needed to know, right?

Here's the tricky thing about dealing with someone like Dad. Yesterday's correct response could be today's red rag to a bull. And he was doing this *now* because he hadn't forgotten about me answering him back that morning. He was petty. *That* at least was consistent. At some level, this was payback brewing.

All I knew was that my preferred Option 3 of screaming in his face was the wrong one. I forced my lips tight shut to stop me doing exactly that, wavering instead between Options 1 and 2. Not wanting an escalation of hostilities.

Too late. It was coming anyway.

Dad took up the chalk and balanced it in his fingers. His mouth twitched. He turned to the board and scrawled another Rule amidst his other angry scribbles and crossings-out and madness:

THE ONLY USEFUL KNOWLEDGE IS THE
STUFF THAT KEEPS YOU ALIVE.

"You don't need to know any of this useless school stuff, Amber. You don't need to waste your time on books. On exams. Bits of paper. Only practical knowledge matters."

It didn't take Dr Freud to work out what was going on.

He didn't like me or Mum or anyone else knowing things that he didn't know. *He*, Ellis Fitzpatrick, was the expert on all matters. Anything else, the actual truth for instance, made him feel inadequate.

"The only useful knowledge is the stuff *I* can show you, honey. How to keep yourself alive, how to fix things, how to provide a clean water supply."

He listed the practical stuff he had me do already. And the things he still wanted to teach me.

How to strip a gun.
How to make traps.
How to break into a warehouse.
How to skin a rabbit.
How to evade capture.
How to snare a looter.
How to do as you're told, Amber.

I was notching them up. If I'd had a special prepper uniform, it would have been covered in tiny fabric badges already.

Dad opened the wood burner and picked up my history folder, scrunching sheet after sheet into a ball and tossing them into the fire. He took my textbook from the table. "This," he hissed, waving *German Social History 1919 to 1989* in my face, "is useless for you now." He ripped the pages out in chunks and added them to the flames. "They tell you lies. It's their version of the past. *Trust no one*."

I swallowed heavily as I stood there watching history burn.

"You learn nothing from history books." He rammed the final pages in and forced them down with the poker. "They don't care about you. I care about you."

I nodded, impassive.

"You're my flesh and blood. Blood's thicker than water."

The rant continued. I switched off, odd words breaking through: blood, water, water, blood.

I thought instead about other book-burners in history. The ones in those very pages disintegrating before me. I forced the tears to stay in my eyes, defied them to reveal themselves.

Dad turned to the bookshelf with my fiction. The handful of books I owned. He wanted me to react. If I showed I cared, he'd won. I didn't ever want him to have the satisfaction of knowing that he'd hit the bullseye. I shrugged.

Reaction.

No reaction.

What did it matter?

All these Rules and there was still no way to win his game.

He took a paperback – *my* book, bought with my money – and forced it into the growing mound in the burner. And another and another.

I said nothing.

As the pages crackled and curled, I *knew*.

His new Rule was wrong but also right, in my topsy-turvy world.

I *had* learned from history. History had shown me. *Where they burn books, they will also ultimately burn people.* That was the Heinrich Heine quote I'd used in my essay. That *was* useful knowledge and it *was* going to keep me alive because now I knew.

I knew that this wasn't going to stop.

He wasn't going to stop.

December

9

After the cupboard incident, Josh caved and took the bottom bunk so I had the double bed. When I wake up in the morning, seeing him all squashed up in there, I feel a teensy bit guilty. His feet are hanging off the end. He slept with the sheet over his head to block out my constant bedside light. My conscience isn't bad enough to make me switch off the light in future or give him back the big bed.

I pick up my advent calendar from the bedside table. Today's door reveals a choirboy singing. His mouth is a perfect O. What's with the ruff? Who makes them wear ruffs and white nighties?

Kev's taking the piss now. First the washing-up, then he's lined up more toilets and bathrooms to clean after breakfast.

Josh says he has a new cunning plan to earn actual cash which doesn't involve clearing up anyone else's bodily fluids. He won't tell me what, because he is exceptionally irritating. He smirks and taps his nose and drags me back towards the Roman museum, turning down towards the coach park.

"Watch this. Americans en route."

A coach is unloading tourists, many in plastic ponchos against the drizzle, wearing baseball hats and trainers. Loud voices comment on the weather and how uneven the 'parking lot' is.

Josh throws his hat on the floor, takes off his parka to reveal his 'I walked the wall' T-shirt and starts singing. I expect it to be terrible, but it isn't. He's good. He taps a drum beat on his thigh and his voice rings out. I don't know the song but it's a folky one about having your heart broken. A group of Americans gather beside him and give him a clap when he finishes, tossing coins and notes into his hat. "I'll take any of those Scottish notes that you can't spend in England," he says, smooth as anything. He nods to me and I gather up the money before it blows away or they realize what he's saying isn't true. I leave a few coins in the hat as a prompt as he starts again. He belts out a country tune that the tourists seem to know and a few clap along while I take the hat along the row.

Too many of them are getting out their phones, recording it. I duck behind Josh, my hood pulled up. "Wrap it up," I whisper. Having Josh tagging along was to make me *less* conspicuous not *more*. Hide and thrive. What was

I thinking? Here we are, potentially being uploaded to YouTube. Josh winks at me. I can tell he's enjoying himself too much. He sings louder and nods at the hat in my hands, raising his eyebrows in an exaggerated gesture. He wants me to go round the group again, getting their money. It's not worth the risk for me and I put the hat on the ground by his feet.

I retreat to the toilet block. I take a cubicle and sit on the toilet with my head in my hands. This is going wrong. I'm not focusing on Dad.

Rule: Stay one step ahead. Focus on the end goal. *Survival is everything.* I wash my hands thoroughly and splash the cold water on my face. I should be back at Beechwood, messing about with the others, finishing the last of our homework before we break up, staying on track for my mocks after Christmas. Instead of this. Hiding in a toilet block in the North of England.

Josh is waiting for me where I left him, now holding two coffees from the van in the car park. The tourists have moved on to the site. "Where did you go?"

"They were filming us," I say. "That's not my idea of being inconspicuous. Hide and thrive, that's the way to go."

"Correction. They were filming *me*. Not *you* in your massive hat and hood. And so what if we pop up on a Facebook page in Minnesota – you think your dad is looking at all worldwide social media posts to find you now?"

"No, but…"

"I know you and your massive scarf are ducking any CCTV. I do the same at times. Even you can't be paranoid enough to think your dad can get access to that, are you? He can't track you."

I shrug. "He taught me to travel like this. To move around the place as unnoticed as possible. And, well, it's not just about my dad. There's his prepper contacts, the police or social services."

"You said no one was looking for you. You didn't walk out of Hogwarts without telling them?"

"No! I left a note. I'm nearly eighteen. It's not a problem."

"It'd better not be."

"I liked your singing," I say to change the subject. "How much did you make?"

"We got forty-five quid for half an hour's work. Americans are the best for giving money. Our notes are like Monopoly money for them." His face is bright and excited. "Forty-five quid, Amber! I'll make a donation to St Cuthbert's, if you like," he says with a smirk. "And we could come back here later, when another couple of coaches arrive."

I've got to admit it's easy money. There's no way I can risk accessing my bank account and giving away my location. My cash reserves are going down. Maybe Josh is more useful than I thought. A good stop-gap between The Haven and wherever I end up – Centurion House maybe?

I blow on the coffee and take a sip. "Why didn't you say you could sing?"

"You didn't ask. Anyway, so what?"

"Why don't you do something with it?"

"What, like record a best-selling album? Don't talk daft."

He counts the money and places it carefully into his wallet.

"Oi. You!" A red-faced middle-aged man is thundering down the path from the visitor's centre. "What do you think you're doing, begging on private property?"

"I was moved by the historical surroundings to give an impromptu concert for our friends from across the Atlantic in the interests of the special relationship," says Josh without batting an eyelid.

The man stops in front of us and jabs a finger angrily. His whole face and neck is gammon pink. "Hawking, begging, busking, impromptu concerts – whatever you want to call it – are not allowed here. So take your girlfriend and get out of here. Get yourself a proper job."

Josh pulls himself up to his full height and Angry Man takes a couple of steps back. "Firstly I do not want a proper job like yours, defined by a uniform of green jumper, brown polyester trousers, a name badge and being rude to people. And secondly, this fair lady –" he gestures to me and I turn away – "is not, and has never done me the honour of being, my girlfriend and we both reject your impertinence for suggesting otherwise."

"Absolutely," I add.

"This may mean that I have to challenge you to a duel," says Josh. "Madam, would you be so kind as to retrieve the gauntlet?"

Angry Man looks nervously behind him for back-up, unsure of what he's got himself into. "Now, hang on a minute," he says. "I'm going to get my supervisor."

"Good idea. You'll need a second for the duel. I'll wait here and limber up." He dips into a deep lunge.

As soon as the guy heads back up the path, Josh grabs my arm and says, "Leg it. You don't want to mess with British Historical Trust."

We put several hundred metres between us and the car park, before Josh collapses in a fit of giggles. "Are we having fun yet?"

"No. Does that happen a lot?"

"Getting moved on? All the time. No matter what I'm doing. I could literally just be reading a book on a bench but looking scruffy. Though that idiot means we'll have to find somewhere else to busk. Rule number one – don't let them get you down. I've found I'm less likely to get a smack in the face if I spout a load of posh nonsense. It messes with their world order – I'm a 'scrounging, homeless druggie' to them but then if I can string a sentence together in a mock posh voice, they're not sure where to place me. I'm messing with their minds." He laughs again, twisting his hands in the air. "All these rules in society we're meant to follow, to know our place. I don't have to do it any more." He turns back towards the hostel. "Take it from me – you don't have to follow all these rules, Amber."

RULE:
I AM THE RULES AND THE RULES ARE ME

When you're at school, it feels like you're always being tested with SATs and mocks and GCSEs. The school's obsessed with league tables and adding value and measuring standards. They go nuts if you wag one lesson or turn up an hour late. They keep an eye on you. That's why I didn't quite believe that no one would check on me when Dad pulled me out of school in Year 10. But, it turned out, all he had to do was send a letter saying he was going to home-educate me and that was it. He signed his and Mum's names at the bottom. I could literally have never been taught anything ever again by anyone and no one would know.

The local authority sent a letter asking to make an appointment to discuss my home education with him but he knew they didn't have a right to pursue it. If he said no (as he did), that was the end of it. I'd seen the letter sitting on the table. And I thought, hallelujah – someone matronly with a clipboard is going to come.

They will see my woefully inadequate father giving me a woefully inadequate education and they will DO SOMETHING.

I was wrong.

No one came.

December
10

Josh leans over me and invades my space with his morning breath and unbrushed hair. "I'm reduced to getting my kicks from whatever tiny picture is in your advent calendar."

"It looks like a jar of ashes today. Cheery."

"It can't be that. Give it here." He squints down at the card. "Must be myrrh or frankincense. That's Christmassy. Always in the nativity play, though I can't tell you what it is exactly, or how to spell either of them. Something smelly and oily?"

"Maybe. Today is a disappointing window. One of life's disappointing days."

"You make it sound like a horoscope, predicting the future."

"Yesterday's picture *was* a choirboy."

"So?"

"And you unveiled your secret singing voice. Mystic. I meant that, as in life, some days are better than others. Occasionally you're pleasantly surprised. Rarely, in my case." I smooth out the card again and review all the windows so far.

"So now your advent calendar is a symbol for life in the twenty-first century."

I shrug. "Why not? Sadly, the signs for how today's going to turn out are disappointing. Must be all the toilet cleaning ahead of us."

We sit silently, contemplating the many ways today might deteriorate and I worry that I've jinxed the day. Until Josh laughs and says, "You're mad, you are. It's just a picture." But he still places the advent calendar carefully back on the bedside table, like a holy relic.

I'm so tempted not to do Kev's list of jobs this morning. I want to look into where Centurion House might be – suss out where the national park starts. But Josh reckons he'll be back here soon and wants to keep Kev's stupid exploitation scheme going. He accuses me of being in a bad mood because I'm not facing up to seeing my dad.

"It's the underlying stress," he says. "Classic. This is exactly why you'd benefit from meditation. You can run from this stuff but you can't hide." He points at my clothes piles. "Like, what the hell's all this about?"

"I'm tidy, that's all. That's a good thing."

Everything has its place. Sets of clothes should be laid out in order, ready to put on in an emergency.

He winks at me then stacks the five piles on top of each other and throws them on the bed. A shoe rolls off on to the floor, the sock missing. I grip the sides of my jeans with both fists to keep my hands still and to stop me wailing at him and jumping straight to the piles to sort them out.

"Try living on the wild side once in a while," he says. "See you downstairs for Kev's tasks. Then we can forage some elevenses in the kitchens."

As soon as he's gone, I scramble to rearrange my kit. I empty out my whole Grab-and-Go Bag. I check and double-check the equipment piles and repack them carefully where they should be. Perfect. And then I realize – I didn't see the rolled-up notes I kept in the pillowcase. I look again, my palms getting sweatier and sweatier. My neat packing thrown all over the place like a jumble sale. I can't find it.

My money's gone.

RULE:
THE ONLY USEFUL KNOWLEDGE IS THE STUFF THAT KEEPS YOU ALIVE

I could forage from an early age – *he* taught me – because those who know the difference between edible and poisonous will survive. Wild food was different from in the States, so he had to learn too. Wild garlic was my favourite. Roasted or nibbled raw. Berries were easy.

Mum and I used to gather sweet, ripe blackberries on the way back from primary school. I'd hand them over with red-stained fingers and we'd make crumble while she told me stories of dragons and magic.

We had a trip once to the beach when I was little and Dad was around. Not for playing beach cricket or paddling like I'd done before with Mum. We met up with another prepper family and had a day of foraging. Seaweed, cockles. We had a fire on the beach in the evening and ate sea beet and samphire with razor clams. That was a good day.

There *were* good days. Days that felt like an adventure.

I tried to hang on to those days when things were bad. When I missed the daylight and my nostrils were full of the smell of stale earth. I tried to remember the smell of the sea and the food cooking and picture the sunset.

Once Dad was back in our lives for good and moving into full-on prepper mode, Mum really struggled. Her memory was shot from the pills she was taking. She tried. Dad would get so impatient and the more he got angry, the more flustered she became. She'd hesitate, looking down at the confusion of leaves and roots and say falteringly, "Yes, edible." Dad rapped her on the head with his knuckles. "Anyone in there?" And she shrank further within herself. "You'd be dead in hours. I've told you this before. Why won't you listen to me? Are you just plain stupid?"

I didn't want to be sworn at, to be dragged by my hair and have my face rammed into rotting fungus, so I learned. Quickly. Some mushrooms are tricky to identify but I would never make a mistake.

Though no one is infallible, right?

December
10

I find Josh pouring chemicals down the disabled toilet on the ground floor.

"Give it back. Now," I say.

"What – the Domestos or the toilet brush? You're very welcome to either."

"My money. You took it. It was my bloody contingency money and you took it."

"I did not! How much? Christ!"

"You took that money from the church. If you're happy to steal from Neville the vicar, from *God*, then why not me?"

"You're way off, Amber. I explained about that church money. A handful of coins – meant for people like me. There's no way I'd nick *your* money."

"The door was locked, Sherlock." I glare at him.

"Kev then? He's got a master key," he says. "Or one of

the other staff. Or people like us, passing through."

"I'm stuffed without that money, Josh." I kick at the plastic bin, knocking it over.

"I wouldn't, Amber, I swear. Search me for it, if you like."

For all his faults, I can't truly believe he'd do it. He *looks* innocent – but then looks are deceptive. *Trust no one.*

"You should always keep your dosh on you in a place like this," he whispers. "Shit like this is always happening."

"Shut up. That's a big help now, isn't it." I flip down the toilet seat and sit with my head in my hands. "I can't report it – I can't get into all that with the police. Kev or whoever have got themselves a windfall."

I check the wallet in my back pocket. "I've literally got forty quid left in my purse. That won't last long. What the hell do I do now?"

"At least I've got some cash. And the busking money." Josh crouches beside me. I feel like punching him. I don't want to be dependent on him. "Consider it a loan if that makes you feel better," he says. "You'd do the same for me."

Would I? I doubt it.

He straightens up the bin and squirts cleaner into the sink.

"Stop, Josh. Stop bloody doing cleaning jobs for this place. Whether it was Kev or some other loser who took my money, this place has had enough out of us."

"Hell, you're right!" He peels off his rubber gloves and chucks them on the floor. A big grin spreads across his face.

"I know somewhere good to sofa surf tonight. Much better than here. I could get us more dosh doing Christmas songs. Pick up some tinsel in Poundland. You could get a reindeer onesie, stick a big red nose on your face. Perfect disguise."

"Very funny. Or there's somewhere I'd been thinking already that I might be able to get my hands on some money. That bug-out place I mentioned earlier – Centurion House – will have food supplies but it'll also have cash or valuables stored there."

"Sure. Just lying around for someone to steal it."

"It's emergency money for preppers. I'm a prepper. This is an emergency."

"I look forward to you explaining all this if we get arrested."

"Sometimes prepping groups share intel and equipment. We came to the Northumberland and Cumbria group once to meet some other preppers."

"Nice. I'll show you mine if you show me yours?"

"It makes sense. Dad went off with them to visit Centurion House while Mum and I stayed with one of the families in a pub with a camping field. It was my twelfth birthday – I remember Mum got the owner to do a cake with candles."

"That's, like, five years ago. What if it's not being used for that any more?"

"If it was as good as Dad said, it probably is. He said it was close by a beautiful water source. Preppers love

112

that. We'd be unlucky to be there at the precise moment a prepper comes to top up supplies but it may have some surveillance and security. We don't just walk up and knock on the door."

"This gets better and better. When we get there, we might not be able to get in. And if we do manage to get in, it might just be full of cans of tuna and emergency camping gear. Where is this amazing place?"

"I'm not sure exactly. I told you, Mum and I didn't go there. On the plus side that means Dad *knows* I don't know where it is."

"On the downside, we're looking for a house that you've never seen but has a starry sky and is near water," he says. "A house that may or may not still be a bug-out house for a bunch of preppers who had an agreement five years ago with your dad."

"It's worth the risk. If it's empty, we could even stay there for a while. It'll have everything we need," I say, feeling more optimistic by the minute. "We'll head towards that national park area via places to kip and keep moving on until we find it. With your local knowledge and what Dad said, we can at least try. Tell Kev we're leaving early. And tell him where to stick that toilet brush!"

———

"Shame you can't drive," says Josh, as the bus is taking forever to get anywhere. "This whole thing would be much easier. And we could sleep in the car."

"Shame *you* can't. You're old enough to have passed your test."

"Too much money. And what's the point?" he says, slouching down further in his seat. "Someone like me would never be able to afford to buy a car or run it."

"Who am I to keep you from the bus network – especially when you're paying for the tickets."

I distract myself with one of Josh's books on the journey to the small town where he's got a mate. Or try to; mostly I just stare at the words or out of the misted-up windows. The roads all look the same, identical villages where nothing is happening and endless moorland. I doze with the motion of the bus and when I next look up we're driving along streets again with rows of shops with their lights beaming on to the wet pavements. It's a bigger town than I expected. Too many people. Too many possibilities of CCTV.

"Curry nirvana," sighs Josh as we pull into the market square. "We can dump the bags at Mo's place, get a takeaway, cadge some beers."

"And use his Wi-Fi to help find Centurion House," I add.

"Sure. I said I was the fixer, that you wouldn't regret having me along. The day is looking up."

But twenty minutes later, when we finally find the place after taking the wrong road twice, Josh's friend doesn't seem that keen to have us staying the night. I sit on the

114

kerb, flicking bits of grit while they argue about it behind me.

"It's only one night, man," Josh is pleading.

"You've said that before. Lola isn't going to like it."

"She won't even know we're here. We'll go out all evening. Back only to kip. We can be gone by breakfast, honest."

"And you've brought someone with you that I don't know at all. How long have you known her?"

"For years, mate. We were in the same foster home way back. She's cool, definitely."

They carry on until at last Josh whistles and I join them. No one is smiling. Awkward. I've heard enough to know Mo isn't going to roll out the red carpet.

"Thanks for letting us stay," I say, through gritted teeth.

"You can have the lounge floor later tonight," he says, as we follow him down the hallway to his ground floor flat. "Do not make a mess. Do not smoke inside. Do not throw up. Do not have sex here. Do not use any of Lola's stuff."

"Rules, rules. So many rules all of a sudden," says Josh. "Chill. You won't know we're here." He puts our bags out of the way by the window and shows me where the bathroom is. "Don't do that freaky clothes unpacking thing just yet," he whispers. "And I think asking to borrow his smartphone is not on the cards."

I use the loo, feeling uncomfortable in this flat where we're not wanted. I pull at my hair in the mirror and plait it.

"Hurry up." Josh knocks on the door and covers his mouth to stifle a laugh when he sees me. "You've gone all Greta Thunberg. Perfect!"

"Perfect for what?" But he's shoved me out the way to take one of his very loud trips to empty his bladder.

I wait, sitting awkwardly on the arm of the sofa instead of taking up room on an actual seat. Mo takes a phone call like I'm not in the room at all. I've become an invisible person.

Josh returns and ushers me quickly out of the flat, calling, "Thanks, Mo. See you later. We're going for a balti."

Something weird is going on because he asks me what the time is twice within five minutes and is walking way faster than his usual speed. Suddenly he stops and grabs my hands. "Don't go nuts, OK? But I have news: I looked it up quickly on Kev's computer at the hostel when he was busy with some guests, otherwise he'd have gone ballistic, and, well, you see…" He swallows heavily.

"What? What are you talking about?"

"Your dad's put in an extra talk date – here. Tonight."

"Are you kidding me? You total…"

"Bus routes – what can you do! Since we're here anyway," he says. "I thought we may as well check it out. You were never going to do this yourself, so I've staged an intervention. You've got unfinished business with your dad. Observe him, see what he has to say. You don't have to do all this running around the countryside looking for bug-out houses. You'll realize he's just…"

"You idiot! You complete idiot! I said no." My heart's racing and my legs feel weak.

Josh's eyes are glinting. He likes the excitement of it. It's more of a game, something to do to fill his usually solitary days. He doesn't know what Dad's like. I've told him some of it, but he hasn't felt it. He hasn't been there. I'm in the same town as my dad. I thought he was miles and miles away.

And Josh has led me here.

I turn back towards Mo's house and my stuff. Josh catches me up on the corner.

"Wait – we're here now. It's late and we've got a place to stay tonight sorted," he says. "We can sneak in at the back. He'll never know."

"You're right, because I'm not going," I say.

"I think you'll see he has no hold over you after all this time."

What does Josh know! He *does*. He does have a hold over me.

I turn to go again but Josh catches my arm. "He's just some bloke, Amber, made of flesh and blood like the rest of us, giving talks on prepping to people who like to grow their own veg in small towns. Honestly, you should lay this ghost to rest once and for all."

He's pressuring me. Have I overreacted to Dad's letter? Could he be a different person? Or maybe *Prep for the worst* means I *should* see what I'm dealing with. I would like to know if he carries any guilt, any trace of Mum. Is Dad as affected as me by everything that's happened?

"I borrowed these from Lola's stuff," Josh says, pulling out a pair of blue-rimmed fashion glasses and a headscarf covered in tiny flamingos from his coat pockets. "You're already very different with the little-girl hair thing. Not at all like your usual look. No offence. Add these – no one will ever know it's you."

I hesitate. Could it work? Could it help me move on with my life?

"All right, I'll try them," I say.

Josh adjusts the scarf and leads me to a shop window to check out the effect. "See, you look cool, honestly. I have a future as a stylist to the rich and famous."

"I look ridiculous," I say. "But I don't look like me."

"So, are we on?" he says.

"I'm not saying yes," I say. "I'll look at the venue and then decide."

It takes a few minutes more to reach the function room in the town hall building, and I feel sicker with every step. Josh checks it out while I wait across the street. I chew my thumbnail and count through the Rules in my head.

Minutes later, Josh bounds back. "It's easy. I've found us a good spot at the back by the fire exit," he says. "The stage is lit so the rest of the room is darker. If we sit at the back he won't see us – too dark, too many people in between.

And you're pretty titchy."

"I haven't seen him since…" I gulp back the memory.

"It'll be fine. He's focused on his talk. And he won't be looking out for you up here." Josh takes my hand. "Even if – a million to one – he sees it's you, he can't do or say anything to you in front of all those people. And he'd have to get through me first. Honestly, you're going to feel so much better. Coming or not?"

The temptation to see for myself what my father's like now is too much. A morbid fascination, like picking at a scab. I push Lola's glasses back up my nose and nod, swallowing hard. We join the crowd going in and he guides me to chairs at the back. We sit, but my right leg jigs up and down with nervous energy.

The hall soon fills and they put an extra row of chairs out. To one side there are emergency packs for sale. Grab-and-Go Bags for the hobbyist prepper. They're overpriced and full of packaging like a Christmas hamper. A thin woman in a camo shirt is pushing them as the ideal present for Christmas. Fire-starter, water filter, energy gel, a torch and emergency meals. Buy three, get a free foil survival blanket. Lightweights.

"This stuff sells," says Josh, watching people queue to pay. "The age of political uncertainty."

I nod. "People who have never thought about it before are suddenly confronted with the reality of a toilet-paper shortage."

"Which scares them, so they need even more toilet paper and so the cycle continues," laughs Josh.

He's trying to make me relax. It works briefly but then the lights dim even more and a man in a red jumper gets up to introduce the speaker and I've only got minutes before Dad arrives. I must stay calm. The intro passes in a blur of praise for my dad and how honoured we are that he's come to this little town from the USA to share his expertise.

Warm applause ripples through the hall and I strain my neck to see him. There he is, bursting with life and energy, bounding along the aisle, shaking hands, patting backs, dispensing 'thank you for coming' and 'good to see you' like a politician. Up the steps, and then his face is in the spotlight at last.

Mr Fitzpatrick the Prepper is on the stage.

His voice is loud and confident. It reaches into the corners of the hall and transports me back like an emotional time machine. I push my toes into the floor, scrunch my hands into tight balls. His exaggerated drawl telling people things they half want, half fear. A flicker of the alternate reality. But I don't know which is scarier – the old Dad or this new, polished one. Which is the more dangerous?

At first, I can't focus on what he's saying. His voice buzzes in my ears. I count through the Rules to settle myself. There's a tightness in my chest. Gradually I calm down and tune back in, force myself to make out the words, to process what he's saying. His voice is familiar but unfamiliar.

"We have gone soft." Dad's voice rings out loud in the hall.

"Yes!" comes a cry from the back.

"We have let *them* disconnect us from the ways of living by ourselves. We have become dependent on others. If you don't know how to feed your family without going to a shop, you need to make a change. You need core skills. Before it's too late."

He moves on to the vulnerability of power and water supplies. Then the SHTF scenario of the collapse of the banking system. People around us who've taken for granted their ability to get their money from a hole in the wall any time they want it, are confronted with the possibility of the total breakdown of the money system within days of a SHTF scenario.

"Your cash and credit cards become meaningless. The control of food will be paramount," says Dad in his new, measured tones. "Don't expect the government to save you. Politicians are in it for themselves. They'll be climbing over each other to get into the Whitehall bunkers while you'll be left out cold in the real world, fighting over who gets to eat a rat."

The crowd shift and murmur. His language is full of words of betrayal, talk of 'the elite' and of 'real people, working people'; smatterings of conspiracy theory. He pitches it as an 'Us' and 'Them' situation where the state doesn't want all of us to survive. "They choose, they set priorities. Do you think you are a priority for them?"

"No!"

More mutterings. More talk of austerity as policy, lack of health resources, of an underfunded civil defence force. Fighting back, battles, enemies of the people. Manipulative phrases fall from his practised tongue.

With one breath he rubbishes experts, but with another suggests himself as the expert voice on prepping. "Biggest crisis facing a generation and are your politicians providing any answers? Or are they scrapping over who gets to live in Number 10 Downing Street or at the White House?"

He produces a yellowed leaflet and waves it above his head. "Protect and Survive. In the Cold War, in the face of the daily risk of nuclear holocaust, your government was advising you to lie in a ditch or get under the kitchen table. Has anything really changed?"

"That's true," says the middle-aged man to my left. "Tape the windows, fill up the bath. Ridiculous. We'd all have been dead."

"Do you think the British Cabinet will be doing that?" booms Dad. "Will they be sheltering under a table or will they be in a state-of-the-art bunker complex? We need to *Prepare* and Survive." He takes the round of applause while nodding and smiling around the hall.

"They've encouraged a climate of 'learned helplessness'," he continues. "All you are fit for is to press 999 or 911 and you expect emergency services to help you. What if they don't come? What if they're not at their post but helping their own families? Are you ready for that?"

He strides across the stage, taking his microphone with him, pointing at members of the audience. "Are you ready, sir?" "Are *you* ready, my friend?" The house lights come up and I shrink into the chair. "What about you here in the front row? Are you prepared? Or are you scared?"

He breathes in deeply. There's a pause. The whole hall is hanging on what he's going to say next. "I want to share a story with you." He speaks more quietly, drawing us in, confiding in us, the special ones. It's a usual tactic of Dad's, copied from his time in the States, practised back at those first prepper meetings.

"United States of America. 2005. Hurricane Katrina. I was there, my friends. Colossal flooding of the levees in New Orleans like it was the days of Noah's ark. Whole districts, whole communities underwater. Do you think the emergency services came to my mother's aid? To my aid? I watched family pets drown, unable to help them. Watched my father take his last breaths clinging to his rooftop while I could do nothing. The government didn't turn up to help in Hurricane Katrina – it was a disaster movie unrolling before my eyes. No power, no transport. Chaos, anarchy, lawlessness. I wasn't ready. I wasn't prepared. Never again, friends. It taught me you can't rely on your government, the politicians, the high and mighty state puppets."

He pauses for breath and a sip of water while his words sink in.

That can't be true – Grandpa was killed in a car accident after too many beers, Mum said. And Grandma's always been alive and well a thousand miles away from New Orleans. But he makes me doubt myself, even though I know he's lying.

"Who *can* you rely on?" asks Dad, leaning forwards towards the front row again, leaving a gap for everyone to contemplate their answer. He taps his temples. "The biggest hurdle, my friends, is up here. In your head. You have to really *want* to survive, *want* to be self-reliant, to pick up the challenges, to take the difficult decisions. Or do you just want to be ordinary, be 'normal' and wait for someone else to save you. Because I've got news for you – *they* ain't comin'!"

"He's good. He's charismatic," whispers Josh. "Even though I know I'm being manipulated, part of me wants to join in too."

How did that happen? My mouth dries as Dad says, "Blood is thicker than water." I worry that he's looking right at me. I adjust my glasses and pull the scarf tighter. Why would he say that? His words are becoming jumbled in my head. Did he just say that about blood and water, or did I imagine it? I mustn't let him into my head again.

He picks up an equipment pack and changes tack. He's talking about practical preparations like an emergency plan for the family, having a Grab-and-Go Bag to get you through the first three days, making links with like-minded individuals, speaking to his colleagues at the end about signing up with prepping groups. He explains how he can generously help us all out with his packs of equipment for a special bargain price, today only, like a smarmy salesman on a shopping channel. He adds how he can help with the restructuring of society after the SHTF. He talks of how we'll need a new way of living for the new reality but he doesn't give the full picture. Doesn't set out in full all his stupid Rules but focuses on the greener ones like *Leave no trace* and developing practical skills to grow food and recycle.

There's standing room only behind us. People clustered in on all sides. My dad has groupies. As he speaks of needing new rules for the new beginnings, there are more cries of agreement. Even an 'Amen'. If the crowd broke out in a gospel choir rendition of 'Hallelujah', I wouldn't be surprised. The hall now has the reverent atmosphere of a church where a preacher is telling his flock the way to the kingdom of heaven.

And they are lapping it up.

RULE:
THE ENDS JUSTIFY THE MEANS

The Rules were being codified. Dad's new project was to put them in order in his tiny writing in the notebook he carried everywhere, then paint them on the walls of the farmhouse in each room, in case we forgot. Like he was Moses and these commandments were revealed to him to spread the Word to the world. He just made them up as he went along, mostly as some freakish power show of how he could force us to do anything he demanded. *Rule: The ends justify the means.* Which meant anything goes. Anything can be justified as a way of getting to the sunlit uplands after the SHTF.

In Dad's world, when he talks about rebuilding afterwards, he *wants* to start again. Have another chance at this life he's failed at so far. He's a nobody now.

He thinks he'll be a somebody afterwards.

He's tired of being a nobody.

He wants to be a somebody at our expense.

Please

Don't

Let

Him

Win.

Dad's speech whirrs around my head all night. I'm glad when daylight finally creeps through the cheap curtains in the lounge and I give up pretending to sleep. I turn off the camping lantern and gather up the takeaway cartons. The beers Josh took from the fridge last night have meant he's snuffled and snored and breathed balti curry fumes. I suppose I wouldn't have slept much anywhere. I just need to get away from here.

There was a minor argument with Mo and Lola at midnight when Mo came into the room for a glass of water and knocked over Josh's half-full can. The spilled beer soaked straight into the carpet like cat pee. Lola went nuts and threatened to chuck us out immediately. Seeing her flamingo scarf and glasses sticking out of my jacket pocket didn't help the situation. I don't like the chaos of Josh's life.

I get why he likes the boring isolation of The Haven.

I use the bathroom as quietly as I can, borrowing Lola's expensive shower gel. I stand under the hot water letting the droplets run down my body as though they can wash away last night's meeting and Dad. It feels like a dream, him on stage. Alive and kicking. The adoration he received, the respect. Why can't people see him for what he is? People just hear what they want to hear. The shower runs cold and I step out, water pooling on the floor in the steamed-up room.

I smooth my skin with Lola's body cream and spray on her deodorant. I sniff at the perfume bottles to make my selection. The strongest scent makes me cough, but I don't care. I want to be cleansed of last night's lies and the lingering memory of dank earth. I want to smell like a different person.

When I creep back into the lounge, Josh has rolled up the sleeping bags and sits rubbing his eyes. "I'm guessing you didn't sleep much after last night?" he says.

"Which is completely your fault."

"Give me a minute to get my gear together. Feels like the middle of the night."

"It's ten past eight already," I whisper, packing my bag.

"You're always looking at your watch," he says, stretching his arms above his head. "You should be more attuned to your body's natural rhythms, not a slave to convention."

"Thanks, Mr Anarchy. How does that square with

your beloved bus timetables? And try to have a day when you don't give me any of your advice. Because it's always rubbish."

"You might not feel better about your dad straight away but…"

"Just shut up, Josh. When you've sorted out your own life, maybe then come and tell other people what to do. I'm getting out of here ASAP. My dad could still be here, picking over the hotel buffet, killing time before his train to the next place. And I think it's time I do this on my…"

The bathroom door slams shut. Followed by some extremely rude words at high volume before the lounge door is thrown open. Lola is shouting in my face before I can get out of the way. She just appeared like a ghost in a billowing nightie. I would never have pegged her as the full-length-nightie type.

"You've been using my toiletries. My expensive perfume. I can smell it on you." She sniffs deeply. No need for her to get so close because I'm literally sweating out her chemical perfumed stuff. But then she grabs my wrist and reaches for my hair to smell that.

She's easy to push against the wall, arms pinned above her head. Weaker than me and restricted by all that fabric, but mainly because she's not expecting it. She's screaming that I've broken her arm but that is plainly just her being a drama queen. If I'd wanted to break any limbs, she'd know about it. I need her to stop all the noise.

"What the hell?" Mo appears in a pair of boxer shorts and starts pulling at me but I'm able to kick him away.

Josh approaches me with his hands out like I'm a wild horse. "Easy, easy."

"She grabbed at me and pulled at my hair," I say.

Lola is still struggling while trying to bite me. Savage.

"Off you get," says Josh, still in his horse-whisperer voice. He takes my hand and leads me towards the door while Mo holds back Lola.

"You're an absolute lunatic," Mo shouts at me.

"She started it. She was in my face about shower gel. *Shower. Gel.*" I want him to understand the unfairness of it all. That I wanted to hit back at her for treating us like something on the bottom of her shoe. That it wasn't OK to sniff me.

"Let's go," says Josh, handing me my bag. He pulls on his trainers while opening the door.

"We were doing you a favour, Josh. All you had to do was follow the rules," says Mo. "And not bloody assault anybody. Don't come again."

I start to say something, but Josh shakes his head at me. "Leave it." He slams the main front door to the flats behind us and storms off down the street, swearing under his breath. At me? At them? At the world?

I catch him up on a damp park bench. "After last night and Dad and everything, I just flipped out."

"You think! It's not like I'm inundated with offers for

places to stay."

"You deserve better friends."

"Because I'm such a catch," he says sarcastically. "Who wouldn't want someone like me rocking up?"

"Just don't end up crawling to people like Lola. We should never have come here."

There's a pause while I assume even Josh is working out I'm talking about seeing Dad last night, more than his sleeping arrangements.

He shrugs. "I guess it's not just you. I wore out my welcome there a while ago. I certainly won't be leaving a good review on Trip Advisor. They can forget that, Amber Warning."

"I don't like sofa surfing," I say. "I don't like owing someone, having to be on my best behaviour."

"Is that why you went through foster homes like they were going out of fashion?"

"Maybe I *like* being on my own," I say. But what was it about *me* that meant I couldn't settle easily into someone else's house and their IKEA back bedroom? I didn't need to sit through all those sessions with Dr Meadows, tight-lipped. I didn't need to give surly responses to Julie across a sticky café table, for her to add to her tea-stained notebook. The answer was obvious. We're all shaped by what's happened to us. However hard we try not to be. However hard we try to bury it. The answer to why I'm such an awkward cow lies in *him*. Dad. Mr Fitzpatrick the Prepper.

"I'm done with staying with people. I'm going to get some camp food and head towards Centurion House. My dad said last night he was headed down south for a few days of talks so I've got a clear window to check it out. I know he won't be with any preppers up here."

Josh gives me twenty pounds. "You get the food and I'll go to the tourist office, get some maps and see if they can help me find it."

"It's not a tourist attraction. It won't have a big neon sign on it saying: 'Centurion House – covert bug-out spot'."

"No – but your dad mentioned the observatory so it'll be in the dark-skies area and he said it had a massive source of clean water nearby. That's enough to start narrowing down the search zone. Let me try – I want to make up for springing the talk on you yesterday."

"There was a Costa café we passed before we got to Mo's," I say. "Near the massive church. I'll meet you outside there in half an hour and then we're going." I hurry away without looking back. It's easier to tell a lie if you don't look people in the face.

"We could pop in Costa for breakfast. Share an egg roll," he calls behind me.

I need to think through last night with a clear head. Without Josh. Horrible as it was to see Dad, I survived, like Josh said I would. I didn't self-combust. And I do know more about what he's up to. Information is *always* good if it helps you prep for the worst.

Last night has left me with something more: I don't want to let Dad win. He was obviously in with the local preppers. So maybe, just maybe, Dad could be using their place to store his stuff from Eden Farm, which gives me another reason for wanting to visit. I saw from the online search that he's been in the States until recently. He must have passed on all the resources from Eden to someone, all his stuff from when we were there. Why not the group he had a link with up here? He had no other family, no friends. He burned all his bridges long ago with the preppers he knew in Wales. If I can get his record of the stress test, I'll be able to have some control.

I get the food I want as quickly as possible – with Josh's money – and pack it away. I won't be comfortable until I'm out of here. It feels like eyes are on me. A girl with a massive rucksack when everyone else is Christmas shopping.

And I won't be meeting up with Josh. I can find my own way to Centurion House. He'll soon get over me not turning up. What planet is he on if he thinks I'm going to sip tea when my dad could still be around?

As I turn the corner, Josh is already waiting outside the Costa, leaning in the doorway of a boarded-up shop, fiddling with his bag. He's not meant to be there for another fifteen minutes. I duck back out of sight. I'll have to find a different way to get to the market square and the buses. I take another look, figuring out the possible routes, but this time I notice that Josh has got company. Two lads are hanging around him, kicking at his bag.

The shorter one spits at him, catching him on the cheek. Josh calmly wipes it off with the back of his sleeve. "Well, I must say that's jolly well not crick—"

Before he can get the words out, the first shove lands on his chest. His normal posh-boy act isn't going to work with these two.

I sigh but I can't just leave him to it. He's like an injured puppy.

The taller one, in ripped jeans and a thin T-shirt despite it being only about five degrees, is unzipping Josh's bag.

"Hey! Leave him alone!" I shout. I stand legs apart, my weight centred, my arms ready to strike.

They look up. The one who spat at Josh breaks into a huge smirk. "Seriously? What are you – thirteen? Your boyfriend is just helping us out with a little question we had."

"Yeah, who the hell does he think he is?" sniggers the other one.

I bet that at least one of them carries a knife as routinely as a mobile phone. And I've already had one fight today. I weigh up what to do. I can't take both of them on. If they lay a finger on me, that's different. But I don't want an 'incident' where the police will come.

The taller one is throwing Josh's stuff out of the bag, laughing at his clothes. He rips a loose cotton target badge off the sleeve of his parka. His books and photos are scattered on to the wet pavement.

"Stop it. Don't say I didn't warn you," I say. I can't bear seeing Josh's belongings chucked around like this. I edge next to him. He's stock-still, like a rabbit in the headlights.

The lads laugh. "Or what? Lover boy will start talking at us again? Hit us with his library book?"

"No. I will first break your nose, then squeeze your tiny little balls so hard that you won't be able to play with yourself for weeks. Make sure that…"

Someone official-looking comes out of Costa, waving a mobile phone. "I don't want any trouble here! If you lot don't clear off, I'm calling the police. That means all of you."

The tall one pats Josh hard twice on each cheek and they run off, laughing.

The man with the mobile tuts. "Clean this mess up," he says to me and goes back inside.

Josh scrambles to pick up the photos and dries them on his front before placing them and his books back in the bag.

"What the hell? Why did you let them do that?" I say. "Two of us, two of them. You were so passive they were always going to take advantage."

"I wasn't doing anything and they laid into me."

"What did you say?"

"Nothing much. Honest. They just felt like kicking the shit out of someone. It's why I don't sleep in doorways. Sometimes I think I'm a stonking great trouble magnet."

"Next time, hit them back."

"I'm not going to be that person." His eyes are filling

with tears. "I'm not going to be like my stepdad, Amber. Ever."

"This is turning out to be a pretty bad day and we've not even been up long. I thought yesterday was bad." I pick up Josh's clothes from the pavement, fold them as best I can and place them in his bag. I don't want to feel sorry for him. It makes it harder to leave him and go it alone.

"Let's do bus roulette," says Josh, sniffing. "The bus that's next to leave the square we get on, wherever it's going. No sneaky looks at a map or the front of the bus. Agreed? Pick a number higher than ten."

"I'm not playing your stupid game."

"All right, I'll pick one. Twenty-one. We get off at the twenty-first stop. That's where we stay tonight. See where it takes us. Leave ourselves in the hands of fate today. What do you think?"

"Is this all a game to you? Me, my dad, those lads who were going to hit you? Look, Josh, I think…"

"Uh-oh. They're back." Josh grabs his bag and pulls me with him towards the street corner. I peep round. The two lads from earlier are back with some mates and a swagger that says there's safety in numbers.

"Shit. They're actually looking for us," I whisper. We run down a warren of narrow back alleys. I'm fitter than Josh though it's tough running with a full rucksack and I don't know my way around this town.

Josh soon has a stitch in his side. "Stop, wait up. Should

we go back to Mo's place? If I can work out where it is from here."

"No. Keep going."

But the alley we're on soon runs out by some wheelie bins and a metal fence.

Josh crouches behind the bins, wheezing. He spits out some phlegm.

"It's better to split. They're looking for us together. Get back to the market square. It'll be busy, full of shoppers," I say. "We'll splash out on a taxi. I'll meet you at the taxi rank." I heave his bag over the fence and give him a leg up.

"But Amber, what if…"

"I'll be fine. They all smoke way too many cigarettes to run fast enough to catch me," I say. "I'll go another way. Go." I push him over and wait to make sure he's OK and running off. I retrace my steps down the alley.

"Well, look who it is!" Two of the lads are coming straight towards me. One of them puts his fingers in his mouth to whistle loudly.

"The girl's over here," the other one shouts.

I have no choice but to head back to the dead end. I drag a wheelie bin towards the fence. They slow down and smile when they see what I'm trying to do. I lift the lid and pull out a broken bike wheel. One moves closer and I hurl the wheel like a Frisbee. It catches him on the side of the head and draws blood.

"Bitch! Get her!" he shouts at the others coming up

behind him.

I climb on to the bin and reach up to the top of the fence, pushing the bin over behind me with a final kick, scattering a foul mess of rubbish. I heave myself over and land on my rucksack like a turtle on a bunch of weeds and tarmac. I'm in a car park for an old industrial unit. I get up and run like I've trained for, and as I reach the edge of the building, I see that the first lad has only just made it over. He's not stuck with a heavy rucksack like me but he's not in shape.

The spire of the big church rises above the row of shops to my left and I run in the opposite direction, towards the strains of Christmas music. I skid into the market square. A brass band is playing carols at the foot of the big Christmas tree and a small crowd has gathered. I push my way through it, feeling the safety of being back in a group.

Josh is at the taxi rank, arguing with a taxi driver through the window.

"I've already told you, I'm booked," he's saying.

"You're not booked. You just don't like the look of me," says Josh. "Your light's still on."

"And now it's off," says the driver, flicking the orange 'TAXI' light. He presses another button and the passenger window starts to rise.

"Leave it. They won't be far behind me." I look across the square. There's a green bus with a queue boarding. "This way! Now."

I slip on the cobbles and swear loudly. In all the rush I

think someone calls my name, but when I turn round I don't recognize anyone in the crowd. My heart thumps. I scan the faces – just normal people doing their Christmas shopping.

"Josh! Come on!" I shout. I'm ahead of him and bang on the bus door as it starts to close, thrusting my arm into the gap. It opens and I pull a panting Josh on board. The door shuts and the bus moves off as the lads enter the square. We sit slumped down on the back seat until the bus has accelerated out of harm's way. I have my hood up again, my back to the tiny camera I clocked fixed by the stairs to the top deck.

Josh holds out his shaking hands in front of him. "Pure adrenaline – look at that. It was like being in that TV programme where they're being chased through the city by hunters. You were amazing."

I'm still uneasy. Did I hear my name called? I wipe at the window, looking through the grime and condensation. The streets are full of shoppers with piles of bags. Festive capitalism in full swing.

No one is coming after us.

I drink some water and share a bar of chocolate with Josh, who's still hyper.

"You realize we are actually playing bus roulette after all. Stop twenty-one here we come," he says, before collapsing in giggles.

I pull out the advent calendar and smooth it down. It's impossible to keep it neat in a rucksack. I count the days left until Christmas. Two weeks. Julie must be having kittens.

Today's thumbnail picture is a Christmas pudding. "I hate Christmas pudding. Does anyone like it? If they did, we'd have it more than once a year, right?"

"Disadvantage – tastes like stodgy mess," says Josh. "Advantage – you can do it in the microwave. Neville the vicar does a nice one."

"Is that where you're going for Christmas dinner?"

"It was OK last year. We had paper hats."

I contemplate the depressing nature of Christmas with a paper hat and a bunch of strangers in the church hall.

"Unless I get a better offer?" says Josh, kicking gently at my foot.

I don't say anything. I don't even know where I'll be by then.

The bus chugs through the town streets, which feel like one big traffic jam. It takes forever, Josh diligently counting stops, but just the ones where people get off, not the ones we sail past. I'm secretly hoping he picked such a high number that stop twenty-one will be back at a depot somewhere and we can abandon this magical mystery tour. But when we reach stop twenty-one, it turns out to be about half a mile beyond a village surrounded by farmland.

When we get off, Josh walks us back towards the village, as if this is exactly what we intended to do. But it's just another sleepy hamlet with a rundown shop and an old-fashioned pub. He holds his arms wide. "So this is where fate has brought us. Pint?"

"No. Looks like the type of place where everyone stares at you when you go in. Where we'd be noticed."

"So? With my amazing good looks, it's an occupational hazard."

He picks up his bag but I don't move. "We've already taken too many risks with other people. No more towns. No more people."

"Oh yes. I forget that social services, the police and every survivalist nutter across the land with access to their own mini poo shovel could be part of the search party."

"If you want to bail on me for the sake of a warm beer, that's fine. But we're sort of foster siblings, remember," I say. "And I got you out of trouble today."

"Good job we're in Nowheresville, I suppose. *We* don't even know where we are, so I doubt anyone else does either." He kicks at the loose stones on the path.

"You wanted to play this stupid game," I say. "Bus roulette. What the hell are you thinking? Who on earth, I mean the whole earth anywhere, who does that?"

Josh starts to laugh. "You're right. Bus roulette – what the hell? I don't think it's going to catch on."

I laugh too. But I stop when I check the timetable pasted up on the village noticeboard. There aren't any more buses in either direction until tomorrow. We're stuck here.

RULE:
THE ONLY USEFUL KNOWLEDGE IS THE STUFF THAT KEEPS YOU ALIVE

Dad had a twinge of guilt after Mum left. He bought a spinning wheel from a junk shop on one of his rare shopping trips. It took up space in the hall that was needed for other things, but it was a 'present' for Mum. To make amends. It was the first time he'd even mentioned her in weeks. No doubt it would soon be followed by a butter churn, I thought. Funny how his plans for a brave new world always seemed to involve strengthening the patriarchy. There was no suggestion that *he* should learn how to shear sheep, spin wool and make jumpers.

"When your mother gets back from ... sorting herself out, she'll need a project. To keep her busy."

Mum could barely settle to thread a sewing needle. She was way too twitchy to spin cloth. Another thing she could fail at and be a perpetual disappointment to him.

First thing she can make is a Gilead uniform is what I didn't say. Instead I said, "We already have enough clothes."

He sighed and dragged his palm across his eyes in a show of exasperation. "We can manage in the immediate aftermath on the items we have already or can forage from abandoned homes or shops. But after that settling-in period, we will need to build our own civilization anew. Reboot."

We both stared at the spindly wooden wheel that was going to spearhead the new industrial revolution. If he was counting on Mum to become the provider of jumpers to a new civilization, he really was deluded.

When Mum never returned, the spinning wheel stayed there, gathering dust.

Stuck in that place like me.

Josh and I huddle outside the closed community shop, while he looks longingly at the window display of Pot Noodles and faded cereal boxes.

"Definitely time to get the camping gear out," I say. "We're going off-grid. No campsites. Most of them are shut in December anyway."

"I wonder why. Could it be because *nobody else* wants to do it?"

"You should have thought of that before your bus bingo. All we need is a building. A farm building – a store, a barn. Anything to keep the wind and rain out. We can make it warm." I lead the way back out of the village, looking for a footpath or overgrown farm track to follow.

I don't want to be too close to a house where we could be spotted. We'll have to light a fire. We haven't seen anywhere occupied since turning off down this track. It's rough, pockmarked with potholes filled with muddy water, which we have to dodge. No tyre tracks.

The light's already failing. We're edging closer to the shortest day of the year. Josh is doing an 'Are we nearly there yet?' in an exaggerated whine. It's becoming rather annoying. I walk more quickly to open up a gap between us. I get my binoculars from the pocket on my bag, ignoring Josh's joke that I'm Action Barbie and he's Librarian Ken. A farm building comes into focus; it might suit.

We climb over the gate, its rusted-up padlock rattling and swaying with our weight. The stone buildings are dilapidated – part filled with plastic-wrapped silage, part with clapped-out farm equipment. I choose the smallest one for our camp.

Josh takes the shovel and toilet roll for some alone time while I set up our stuff. Whatever its shortcomings, this place wins hands down for me over Mo and Lola's flat. If it was summer, I could've done more sleeping out and not risked any towns at all.

Josh stumbles back and I throw him the hand-cleanser gel.

"Why are you moving everything about?" he says. "Do you have to tidy everywhere we go?"

"It's full of combustibles and I'm also thinking of ventilation and the risk of carbon monoxide poisoning."

"Great. I knew I needed yet another reason to hate

camping." He pulls up a crate to sit on and pads it with a jumper.

"There's a hole in the roof which should carry away smoke and gases if we keep the door ajar to get the air circulating."

"Amber. I'm just thinking that maybe you're not a traffic light warning of danger after all. Maybe you're moving towards another meaning."

"Fossilized tree resin?"

"I was going to say a semi-precious gem. I mean, look what you've done with the place!"

With my knife, I cut swirls of curled bark from the saplings by the gate to use as dry tinder. I gather the driest sticks I can find and arrange them in a tepee shape to build the fire. Josh hands me the old newspaper he picked up on the bus and I rip off strips.

"You're so good at all this camping stuff," says Josh, getting in the way.

"It's not camping. It's basic survival. Shelter, water, food. There are multiple ways I can get a fire going and you'd be amazed at my water collection and purification knowledge."

"Nothing about you surprises me any more. Heard of a tap?"

"For someone with no permanent home, you're pretty confident that you'll always have access to a flowing tap. You can manage weeks without food but only three days without water. What about now?"

He waves his water bottle. "This. Rain, streams, tap at a building somewhere."

"What if the water's cut off or there's a dead sheep upstream? You can't waste fuel and time boiling water to drink. I've got purification tablets. My bottle has a built-in carbon filter. At a push, I could use solar disinfection. Pick up a disease or stomach upset with no medical care – that could be fatal."

"You're such a little sunbeam."

"A pragmatist."

"Pessimist. Can't you lighten up? I'm beginning to understand why you're…" He pauses.

"What? What am I?"

"Nothing. Never mind. What else do you know how to do?"

"Basic power generation. Don't say it – there's a switch for that."

Josh smirks back. "There usually is. Granted not in our current deluxe accommodation."

"Even a mobile diesel generator only lasts as long as you can get the fuel. I could rig something up with an improvised wind or solar source. Big cell batteries – like the ones in golf buggies – are what you're going to need to store the power."

"All right, Einstein," he says. "Do you want me to rub two sticks together to light the fire?"

"If it makes you happy."

I let him struggle for a few minutes, smiling to myself, before I toss a box of matches from my bag at him. "I don't want to spoil your fun but I usually use one of these."

I rig up my mini camp stove on a large stone and hold up two packets of food. "Chilli or curry? They taste the same."

"I'll go for chilli. I think I've had enough curry after last night. Though I'm not going to lie – I'm glad you're not trapping and skinning a badger or something else cute and furry for food. I did wonder."

"I've had my eye on that wood pigeon in the rafters. If we were here longer, I'd make a snare. I've got the wire."

Josh is wide-eyed. "To catch the pigeon? You can't do that. Quit acting like Bear Grylls. It's freaking me out."

"You're about to eat a beef chilli."

"It's not the same. You can't murder a *pigeon*. That convenience store will open in the village tomorrow."

"All right. At the moment we don't need to kill anything."

"Well then, don't."

I could describe in great detail how the first time you kill something is the worst. But I hold back because I don't want to tell him that the revulsion at trapping a squirrel or gutting a trout wears off. That over time you can learn to butcher a deer without flinching.

That I've learned that you can get used to anything at all.

The gas flickers on and heats the water while I tend to the fire. The wood crackles and I fan the smoke from the damp wood.

"I suppose, it's kind of impressive having all these skills," says Josh. "Not how to eat a hedgehog so much – but these pre-digital technologies like building a fire."

"It could save my life. Not just because I can do this survival stuff but because I have a set of skills. *I'm* the one people will want to keep alive."

"But you'd still have a massive store of food?"

"Of course, and equipment. That's the main thing preppers focus on – stockpiling supplies. But you don't put all your eggs in one basket. You split your supplies, hedge your bets, in case you get raided. Plus, you have somewhere planned to relocate to like Centurion House – a bug-out place, usually remote or well hidden and more secure, where you can survive the emergency. You accept that you're a potential target for those who haven't prepared. But you do have a lot of food to eat while you're waiting for the hordes to attack. That's a classic prepper joke."

"Hilarious."

"The UK doesn't really have the same 'escape to the wilderness' options as the States or Canada. Though over there you've got the added danger of well-armed fellow citizens. If you haven't got your own place, solar panels or wind turbines could all be signs of a bug-out house, which will have a store nearby, possibly underground. Look out for blackout blinds, lack of lights and movement."

"Weird that all this is going on out there. People preparing for something that might never happen.

A strange way to live."

"And yours isn't? Why do you live like you do – moving on all the time?"

He shrugs. "I don't like the alternative much. You should see some of the places they've offered me. This is often better. Safer."

"Mum and I once lived for three days in a multi-storey car park when we thought Dad would be looking for us. There was an overhanging section by the ramp where we sheltered, and we took a load of cardboard from outside the back of Waitrose…"

"Classy."

"Thank you. And during the day we sat in the library. I washed my hair in the tiny sink in the toilets and used the hand dryers."

"Love a good library," nods Josh.

"Mum stopped taking her meds. She…"

I stop. I'm oversharing. Even with someone who's been there, done that. It's too personal.

"Anyway, we couldn't stay there," I say. I add the boiled water to the dried food and stir. It's fuel, not a gourmet meal. I give the bulk of it to Josh, the human dustbin. "Eat up. Hot food gets cold quickly in the fresh air." Sitting here with Josh, looking into the fire, life feels under my control again. Using my skills to keep myself safe. Prepared. Not scared.

Josh speaks through his mouthfuls of food. "I don't think

the rat race is for me. Rubbish job for rubbish wages to live in a rubbish house. What's the point? Nothing they offered me was anything I wanted to do. This is better, believe me. Freedom."

"No money."

He shrugs. "I get by. You need less to live on than you'd think. Might go and work on some eco farms in Europe this summer, for rent and board. Go back down to Somerset to pick a few apples. Or help on a project I know up in the Cairngorms. Read some books. Busk. There's stuff to do, ways to live that don't make me feel like I'm suffocating. I prefer that no one – except you – knows where I am and what I'm doing tonight. After all those years of feeling I needed to fill out a form in triplicate to take a pee, this is better. I'm not good with people telling me what to do – which rules out most jobs."

I get it. But I think I *do* want to belong somewhere. Now I've had a taste of it.

"You can always come with me, picking apples or whatever." He looks down, embarrassed. "Only if, you know, you want to, like."

We sit around the fire, warming our toes and talk. I get out my wind-up radio and pick up a selection of hits from the nineties. I ask him about his grandma. She looked after him until she became ill and he got taken into care. He shows me a couple of photos and then neatly places them in the pages of his book again. He carries his family history around with him in those pages.

I tell him more about my dad. Not all of it – the edited version.

He gets it. He gets why I haven't said anything to Julie or Dr Meadows or anyone at school. He gets why it's more complicated than someone who hasn't ever walked in our shoes would think. He listens carefully, poking at the fire with a stick. "Sorry if I pushed you into your dad's event last night. I honestly thought it would help."

"It was weird. Seeing him but not seeing *him*. He can be different people. Take on a character when he has to. It wasn't how I expected."

"How are you going to stay out of his way? Live wild forever?"

"Says the man who manages to do just that."

"It wouldn't suit you. You've got things you want to do, I can tell. Mainstream. Try doing anything 'normal' without a fixed address, without somewhere to get a good night's sleep or wash your clothes."

"I'll have options, once I've dealt with the whole Dad situation."

"Now I've seen him in the flesh, got to admit I was impressed," he says. "And he didn't look like a quitter."

And that's what's been unsettling me. Josh is right. Dad looked like someone who gets what he wants.

A noise wakes me and I and sit up quickly. The light from my camping lantern shows Josh thrashing around in a nightmare. He shouts out again.

"No, no, no." Josh bangs the side of his head with his palms. "Stop. No, no."

I wriggle over in my sleeping bag and grab his hands. "Josh, it's fine. It's a bad dream, that's all."

But he's sobbing. Gasping for air like a small child. It scares me. I don't know how to make it better.

"Shh. I'm here with you," I say quietly. I wrap my arms around him and lay my head against his chest, feeling him trembling. I've been so focused on my own past, I haven't paid any attention to his and how come he's in this situation. He's bone-brittle beneath his normal bluster and non-stop talking.

"Shh. I'm here. It's OK," I say and slowly he calms down and his breathing steadies. His sobs subside and eventually he relaxes.

"Don't leave me," he blurts out.

"I'm not going to leave you," I say. "I'm right here."

He hugs me back, resting his chin on the top of my head.

"Promise? Do you promise me?" he whispers. "You won't let me down?"

I nod, hoping that I'm not the latest in the long line of people who've broken promises to Josh.

But knowing that I am.

RULE:
ALWAYS HAVE YOUR GRAB-AND-GO BAG

Our Grab-and-Go Bags had to be checked every Sunday. Ordinary people play football or have a lie-in. My Sunday morning began in front of my unpacked kitbag arranged in rows exactly the way Dad liked it. He went through his checklist and made ticks in his notebook.

So long as I was within an hour of it, I could leave my bag in my room. Dad's lived in the back of the van. The petrol tank was always at least two thirds full.

I was pitifully grateful at the time that I only had to go through that rigmarole on Sunday mornings and could then slide the bag back into the wardrobe where I couldn't see it. It was a reminder of all the bad SHTF stuff awaiting me in the future.

At least I didn't have to lug it around school. Because nothing screams social suicide more than carrying a camo kitbag everywhere.

Dad split the world into preppers and non-preppers, like wizards and Muggles in Harry Potter. He said the fewer locals who knew we were preppers, the better. I didn't argue with that. My cool rating was low to begin with. I didn't want kids from school to see how I lived, to tell everyone. I was already the odd girl in the class, always reluctant to accept any invitations because I didn't want to have to return them. What if they saw the spare room lined with neat shelves of provisions when the rest of the house was a dump? Or if Dad suddenly required me to pluck a roadkill pheasant on the kitchen table? Or he screamed at Mum for not being able to operate a CB radio? Because even though it was *our* normal, I increasingly knew it wasn't other people's.

Nothing about us was normal.

Dad's reason for seclusion was a paranoid one: having other people over was too risky. They'd be bashing our door down after the apocalypse if word got out that we were the only household for miles around with a clean water source, fuel or antibiotics. And, worse, who knew what would happen if we had visitors at the exact moment that we had to go, go, go. We couldn't take them with us, share our vital food resources, jeopardize ourselves.

Dad had a small list of other people he was prepared to help, but when he pulled me out of school and we moved to the farm, we lost the few people I was still allowed to see. I was just fifteen and had no one any more. Dad's list grew even shorter.

Mum got struck off the list shortly afterwards when she had to get her head together away from him and didn't come back. She was a liability rather than an asset. A colossal overhead. Her neediness could compromise our security. He sat me down and said all that.

That was his big excuse for not getting her back. I guess he really meant all that stuff about blood being thicker than water. I was his flesh and blood. Mum was just a failed relationship. A reminder of his failure.

I kept myself going by repeating that it would pass. All this would pass.

The list had got shorter until it was whittled down to him and me.

Possibly just him.

December

12

The cold wakes me up. I start the fire for warmth and set up the stove to boil water for tea. My head's throbbing and I'm shivery. I want to crawl back into my sleeping bag. After a quick wet-wipe wash, I put on my warmest clothes. They all feel damp. I'm burning up. Hot and clammy. I *can't* be ill. Not out here.

Josh hears me groaning and feels my forehead with the back of his hand. "Your face is the warmest thing in here." He makes no mention of his nightmare or night terrors, whatever the hell they were. Maybe he doesn't even remember them. "Let's check the all-seeing advent calendar," he says. "If it's something alive like a reindeer, you're going to live. But if it's another urn of ashes like the day before yesterday..." He draws a finger across his neck and makes a gurgling sound. "And the winner is..." He fumbles with the card and laughs. "Uh-oh. It's a wreath."

"Great. Like you'd put on a grave."

"This one *is* jolly – with a bow and ribbons and pinecones. More for a front door. A festive front door. Definitely not a grave. Or a coffin. Much."

I build up the fire, hoping I'll feel better with some heat. I scrunch up pages from the newspaper again. My eye is caught by the photo on page five. It shows a man in a hospital bed with two black eyes and a face so swollen even his own mother wouldn't recognize him.

LOCAL VICAR LEFT FOR
DEAD FORGIVES THUGS

WARLEYDALE vicar Rev Neville Shipley is recovering in hospital after being callously beaten by two men who broke into the vicarage next to St Cuthbert's church.

The popular local clergyman was attacked when he confronted the two masked men on the evening of 9th December. They took personal items including his laptop and family valuables.

"I forgive them," said Rev Shipley from his hospital bed in Royal Victoria Infirmary. "They must have been desperate to do such a thing."

The clergyman could have been further injured if the thieves hadn't been disturbed by the arrival of four choir members.

Rev Shipley refused to speculate as to whether the

perpetrators could be users of the popular drop-in service for those in need that he runs every week. It has previously attracted criticism as a 'magnet for undesirables', according to a local resident who wished to remain anonymous.

I inspect the beaten-up face in the photograph. It *is* him. It's Neville the vicar. So much for God and the angels helping him out in his hour of need. I pass it to Josh.

"Lowlifes," he says. "I'll have to visit him when he's home. Do you think he'll still be hosting Christmas dinner?"

"You're all heart. Your first thought is your own stomach."

"There are some messed-up characters at his drop-ins but I'd never have thought they'd do that to him. Poor sod."

"You don't think..." I begin. "Never mind."

I stand up but sway and sit down quickly.

"You look rough," says Josh. "Maybe the balti the other night didn't agree with you? My guts were a bit ropey yesterday."

"That curry was over a day ago, though food poisoning can manifest within any period from hours to many days depending on the kind of infection."

"What's that? Page thirty-two of the prepper's first-aid manual? I thought the place looked a touch dodgy but you were in such a state after the talk you obviously needed comfort calories quick."

"I don't have the symptoms. It's just the start of a cold or a bug."

"Luckily we don't have to be anywhere today," he says. "That's the beauty of life on the open road – we can please ourselves."

"By hanging out in a random cowshed, with a temperature."

"I'll go through the freebie leaflets and maps I picked up at the tourist office. They cover the national park area and Kielder Water north of Hadrian's Wall. Who needs Google when you've got your own brain? They're not as detailed as a commercial map, and are obsessed with where you can go for a cream tea, but I should be able to narrow down the search area. You can be on bed rest. Haven't you got enough food in that bag of yours to keep us going?"

Is it all right to step down for a day? To let someone else 'look after' me? Survivors are meant to have a positive mental attitude at all times, however they're 'feeling', but I so want to sleep and get rid of this fever.

"There's no way your dad or social services or Father Christmas himself is going to know you're here. *We* don't even know exactly where we are, says Josh, plumping up my pillow. "I'll do a walk back to the village, get the name of the place, work out the bus routes. You take the day to feel better. Get rid of the temperature. Pop a pill from your massive first-aid bag."

He zips me back in my sleeping bag and is generally ten times more helpful than he's been since I met him – which makes me think he does remember what happened last night and he's trying to repay the favour.

Rule:
Prep for the Worst

I was the only fourteen-year-old kid expected to do car maintenance on a school night, and one time I caught my hand with the wrench when doing an oil change on the van. I instinctively cleaned the cut, sprayed it with antiseptic and inspected it. In a post-antibiotic world, this kind of injury could kill you. So I took it seriously. Dad had trained me to take it seriously. When the SHTF, we'd be the end of the line for our own medical care. I'd done 'courses' in treating injuries and hygiene-related issues like rehydration and food poisoning. Mum was meant to have a handle on midwifery and natural pain relief, and Dad had nailed emergency dentistry and medication. So now I welded my cut together with steri-strips. Neatly done.

We had a supply of antibiotics and other prescription drugs if I needed them. Dad had methods for getting them prescribed when they shouldn't have been so he could build up a stock. We switched between doctors, made appointments with the most junior ones or locums. Dad picked appointments when they'd be tired and rushed at the end of the day. At the slightest sign of a sore throat, Dad had me screaming myself hoarse into a folded towel to inflame my tonsils ready for inspection. I'd lie to the doctor that I had a fever, that it had lasted for days.

The antibiotic, or whatever, would be added to the refrigerated drugs store or to the locked drugs box, depending on type; job done.

Looking back, it's odd, right? If I had told any one of those doctors what was really happening, maybe they'd have taken me away from it all, way before Dad dragged me to the farm in Wales and I wasn't allowed to see anyone any more, let alone a health professional who worked for the state. The doctor could have ushered me into the arms of someone like Julie. Got my dad locked up.

I could have saved Mum.

I could have saved myself.

December
13

I feel better when I wake up. Hungry. Feeble, but with no temperature. I take it slowly getting ready but I know I can move today – I'll be able to head further towards Centurion House.

To his credit, Josh is already up, keen to show me his 'homework' as he calls it. He's identified a large area between the dark-skies observatory and a massive reservoir, and worked out how we get there.

I set about brewing nettle-leaf tea as a thank you. But I don't think he's impressed.

"Nettle tea and soup are my signature dishes. Nature's free superfood. Better if we had some honey to add. They're not as sweet this time of year and a bit withered, but there's still enough of them out there."

"Yes, waiting to sting me when I went for a pee."

"Dad used it like a test. Whether Mum *believed* him enough to pick the nettles. By that stage living on the farm, she was scared of everything. The funny thing about nettles is, if you grasp them firmly and quickly, they don't sting." I mash at the green clump in the kettle. "But if you try to avoid getting stung and are too timid, they'll get you. It'll sting like hell."

"So happy my own cuddly little Bear Grylls is back," says Josh. "Any idea how boring it is out here with no one to talk to? And nothing but freeze-dried camp rations. Any longer and I'd have had to eat you." His scraggly beard has sneaked up on his chin over the last couple of days and his hair could do with a cut, but I kind of like it as it is.

"Boredom is a danger after the SHTF," I say. "You need to stay switched on. That's why you should keep learning stuff, play cards, whatever. And we've only been here two nights. Not a long stress test."

"If you mean, am I stressed? Yes. I don't like looking after a sick person in a cowshed. That's beyond my pay grade. Especially in December. We should splash the cash on a B&B tonight. Use my busking money."

"Some preppers say we should all be stress-testing regularly, like, spend twelve to twenty-four hours without power and try out what you'd do. There was a Swedish experiment a while back that tried it with a bunch of people." I hand him a mug, which he sniffs hesitantly.

"Gran talked about the power cuts in the seventies and

how they sat around with candles and sang songs by the piano," he says. "She made it sound quite cosy."

"The novelty would soon wear off in the modern world. Things you take for granted simply wouldn't function. Petrol station pumps don't work, or banking and cash tills. Nothing can be recharged. All those people addicted to smartphones that you go on about, they'd be stuffed. Air conditioning, heating, life-support machines, operating-theatre lighting, sterilizers – what would you like to live without? Even for twenty-four hours."

"But they have back-up systems and generators, right? Hospitals would be OK."

"Maybe. Back-ups are only directed at the vital services – not at keeping you and your home ticking over. And they've found they can't really run stress tests in real time – too risky. They use simulations, war-game scenarios on paper or with algorithms. And that British Blitz spirit they like to bang on about, turns out to be in short supply."

I pick up the advent calendar. It's the thirteenth – unlucky for some.

"Remember the Asda riots over discounted televisions on a Black Friday sales day?" I say. "That showed the hard truth of the modern-day Blitz spirit. Every man for himself. Or for a cheap TV set. Anything longer than twelve hours without services runs the risk of major civil unrest." I pick at the thirteenth door, located on the tummy of the largest polar bear. Today reveals two bells and I flick it over to Josh so he can see.

"I suppose half a day is how long people last before going nuts about not having access to their Instagram," says Josh.

"That Swedish group went from cheerfully eating pickled herring sandwiches together to *Lord of the Flies* really quickly," I say. "Some think a major change would be a chance to rebuild a common urban future, sharing skills to make a new happy-clappy community life. There's some overlap between green activists and preppers, for sure. But Dad always taught me that when the chips were down it would be all about self-preservation and anything else was hippy fantasy. That's why he wanted us to be ready to fight off anyone. Prepared. Not scared."

I lay out my kit ready to pack it back in the bag neatly. *Everything has its place.* And bag up our rubbish. *Leave no trace.*

Josh picks up the leaflet from St Cuthbert's, and looks at Dad's talk dates that I scribbled on the back.

"We should see where all these other places he's going are. It's an easy way to keep track of him."

"I'm not going to another of his talks, thanks. Though you're right, it means we know he's not in *this* area. We're not going to find him arranging cans of baked beans at Centurion House."

"Ah – I've been thinking while you've been poorly. I got to pondering what you said about your dad taking on a character. It's funny how he's doing all this in a short space of time. Intensive. Looking at all these dates now, there's nothing before mid-November. Nothing after December twentieth, or scheduled for next year. Why?"

"Maybe he's going back to the States for Christmas," I say hopefully. "Doing more over there again."

"We didn't see that on the social media stuff. He didn't mention it at the talk. And if he's such a big cheese and he plainly enjoys whipping up a crowd, seems funny that he's not doing more of it. Pass me your map of the UK."

I give Josh the map and he pins it up by pushing it on to a couple of rusty nails on the wall. He circles the locations of Dad's visits in red pen.

"This is a waste of time. You're mucking up my map." I try to take the pen off him, but he holds it high above his head.

"I'm Sherlock Holmes and you're Dr Watson in this scenario," says Josh. "You're the sidekick, doubting my brilliance. Now stand back. Look at all the red marks. What do you see?"

"An expensive map you've just ruined."

He turns his head from one side to the other. "Looks like they're in clusters. Circles of events in certain parts of the country. Why group them so close to each other? Wouldn't he get a bigger and better audience if he spread them out across the country, or went to bigger cities?"

"True. Whole regions of the country are missed out," I say, tracing lines between places with my finger. "This bit in Carmarthenshire, that's where Eden Farm was, the last place we lived together. This cluster in South Wales – that's where we lived before the farm. The school I went to until Year 10 is just about here." He marks it with an 'S' on the map.

"He definitely knows other preppers in that area," says Josh. "Makes sense to go back there. He's got a network, people who will attend a talk. But what about all these talks in Somerset?"

The dots are more scattered there. "We lived in this place when I was little. And here when Dad moved back from the US before we went to Wales." Josh marks more 'S's for the schools I attended and draws little houses where we've lived. "Bath's where Mum and I ended up sleeping in the car park." That gets a tiny drawing of a house.

"And here, drumroll…" Josh says, drawing another house with a door and two windows, "is where you were in the foster home with Phil and Sue. And me. Where's your current school?" He hands me the pen. "And anywhere else you were in a foster home."

I add more letters.

Dad's talks are circling the area.

"Ever go on a holiday? Memorable day trips?" asks Josh.

I add some 'H's to places in South Devon and the Welsh coast. All have red dots already from Dad's talks.

"Your mum's family?"

"Her parents died when I was just a baby. I don't remember them at all."

"Where did they live? If you were going to go back to see their old house, their graves – where would you go?"

"It was in South Wales, near the sea. Somewhere beginning with a double L. That's all I can remember. I know that doesn't narrow it down much in Wales."

"By the magic of red dots, I'm betting it was here." Josh taps at a lone red mark. "Kind of a small place for your dad to bother with."

Josh's enthusiasm at what he's revealing is giving way to my slow sense of dread.

"All we have to do is join the dots, so to speak," he says. "Is he just visiting places where he knows he'll have an audience?"

"No," I say quietly. "You're right. He's systematically going to places *I* have a connection with." The red dots leap out at me from the map. "He's trying to flush me out."

"OK. You win. Your dad *is* a psycho," says Josh. "Though some people could see it as a loving father leaving no stone unturned to find his estranged daughter."

"There are places on there he didn't know about. My current school, Phil and Sue's…"

Josh shrugs. "Maybe he's just lucky with those happening to be in the area you've already been associated with."

"He knows now that I was under Somerset Social Services. He sent them a letter. Mum had always been deliberately vague about his details when she spoke to them."

"Mind you," says Josh. "Why did he add in the talk *we*

went to? Was your only visit to Northumberland that trip when you were twelve?"

"Yes. So that country pub Mum and I went to can't be too far from the location of that talk and Mo's house. And Dad went from there to Centurion House on his day trip."

"Your dad is thorough. Doing a talk up here because of a short trip, five years ago."

"Obsessive, not thorough."

"And he knows there are interested preppers up here," he says. "We saw them there, selling the kits, signing people up for info."

"This means going to Centurion House could be riskier than I thought," I say. "We'd have to be really careful approaching it. Check no one is there."

I haven't told Josh that it's not just about the cash and a bug-out place to use. If there's the slightest chance that Dad's records – minutely detailed stupid, stupid records – are there, it's worth it. It could be a way, the only way, to get him out of my life forever. That footage could be my insurance policy.

I nudge Josh. "So are you still coming to help me find my needle in a haystack?"

Josh sighs again and takes down the map. "Lucky for you, terrible life choices are another of my specialities. Anyway, we might see a red squirrel up there in the forests. They're protected. I need to come to stop you turning one into a kebab."

RULE:
EVERYTHING HAS ITS PLACE

When he moved us to the farm, Dad could do so much more than he had at our old conventional house. He could go all-out survivalist. We called it a farm, but it was really a tin-pot smallholding, too remote and ugly for the average hobby farmer who wanted to keep alpacas. The nearest shop was fifteen long miles away, and it was rubbish. Even I could see this was not prime agricultural land, going by the weeds poking out from the stony fields. It was bleak, plagued by miserable weather. The whole area was only fit for grazing sheep.

But Dad wanted a place where we could dig in and be self-sufficient. Somewhere we could survive after any emergency for months or even years. Hide and thrive. It had to be off the beaten track, well above sea level, away from centres of population that might make demands on it. Away from the collective that he was rapidly falling out with, thanks to people getting hacked off with his self-appointed dictatorship.

Dad got another pile of money from Grandma. Maybe she thought he'd use it to visit her. Spend it on her granddaughter's education. Or well-being.

Or maybe she hoped it would keep him away.

The landlord was happy to leave us alone and do everything off the books. He was obviously delighted to get some value out of an unwanted place that no other family would pick. He pocketed the rent Dad handed over before we could change our minds. He sped off in an ancient Land Rover, kicking up dirt on the track, with my idiot father thinking that he'd got the better deal. Dad dusted off the broken wooden sign that said: 'EDEN FARM' and fixed it up.

Eden! Dad took it as a sign that we'd come to the right place to build a new way of living. Paradise. Mum took it as a sign that she couldn't cope with anything any longer. I took it as a sign that the universe was having a good laugh at my expense.

Eden Farm wasn't the preppers' paradise Dad had billed it as. It was back-breaking work to plant crops in the ripped polytunnel. We were too late in the season. It was too dry. The seeds wouldn't germinate. The soil was poor. The sloping field faced the wrong way. We had no experience of farming. There were only two of us to work. Mum had let us down. There were a hundred different things for him to rant about and blame.

We set up the usual supplies store, unpacking our previous one from his flatbed van. *Rule: Everything has its place. Cans and jars should face forwards and be exactly one centimetre apart.* The outbuilding he'd earmarked was full of leaks and rats. I added washing off rat wee and droppings from jars and cans with nibbled labels to my daily list. I hated those rats.

Without the help of the collective, we didn't have the same access to resources and discounts and shared provisions. Grandma's money was quickly evaporating even though we had nothing of any use to show for it.

Even the local wildlife knew we were amateurs. A fox took half our chickens in broad daylight. Dad fired his shotgun but by the time he'd gone and got it, the damage was done. He caught the fox on its back leg as it fled, leaving a disgusting trail of blood, guts and feathers behind.

One day he announced that we'd grow peaches.

"I like a fresh peach for breakfast, baby girl."

We had tinned peaches lined up, one centimetre apart, facing forwards, already in the store. We were on the hillside, the Welsh hillside, average July temperature sixteen degrees.

"Aren't they for hot countries. Can you even grow them here? Are they trees or bushes?"

"Trees!" he snapped. "We'll plant a mini-orchard of peach trees."

That sounded expensive, long-term and futile. The perfect project for Dad. Like so many things in my life, this wasn't about peaches. It was about obedience, the Rules. It was him telling me I'd still be here next harvest, picking at dead fruit trees.

Something about the stupid peaches made me cry. I knew it was a stupid idea. He knew it was a stupid idea, deep down.

And yet, he said it.

Another test where I must give the right answer, repeat the correct lines from the script, be obedient, compliant.

Believe in something stupid.

So I nodded. I added peach trees to the list of pointless, impossible tasks and muttered, "Great idea, Dad," while he smiled at me and I tried to be accepting and to believe, for an easier life.

On the outside at least.

Inside was another matter.

─────●─────

By one of those strange laws of the cosmos, just when I thought things couldn't get any worse… Surprise! They did. Dad and I were foraging for mushrooms one day, working in the steep woods towards the edge of our land. We stumbled across an entrance to a cave, overgrown and entangled with brambles. We must have walked past it hundreds of times before. He ignored the broken '*Danger!*

Keep Out!' sign swinging on one screw from the iron gate, and the stink of fox poo and dank earth, and forced his way in. I waited outside but he was soon back for me, flushed and excited, pulling me in to explore, using his torch as we went deeper.

The cave was a disused store. Bricks and timbers had been used to reinforce the three rooms or chambers that grew darker and smaller as you got further from the entrance. There had been gold mines not too far away in Roman times; maybe someone had tried their luck here, or hollowed out a limestone cave to quarry the rock. A heap of ashes and scorched walls showed someone had used it in the last few years – maybe kids from the farm long ago. Though I couldn't imagine a worse place to hang out.

Damp, dark, enclosed.

That place was all my worst nightmares rolled into one.

"It's perfect," said Dad. "Perfect."

That was his new project. Worse than the peaches. He didn't want our new find as another storeroom. He wanted it as a bunker. A bunker in the bowels of the earth that we could retreat to if the shit hit the fan.

"We've found our own secure escape spot. Just waiting for us here. Like a sign. From the universe."

I was sick of signs, wherever they were from.

His eyes gleamed and he immediately set about sorting it and preparing, making detailed plans in his spidery writing. Sketching out how it would work. He dragged out the rusted set of gates, which he could paint, rehang and padlock.

He just needed a trusted workforce to clean it up.

That turned out to be me.

He made me swear never to tell another living soul about it. Not even Mum.

That was easy to promise because I didn't even know where she was. She'd been gone for weeks.

I promised.

He handed me his knife.

It was a blood oath. As usual, only my blood was spilt.

```
┌─────────────────┐
│  December       │
│                 │
│      14         │
│            ◹    │
└─────────────────┘
```

The advent calendar's getting tatty from so many moves.
But nowhere feels like home until I've set it up, finding a
shelf or windowsill to rest it on. It puts our mark on a room.
This may be a bed-and-breakfast twin room smelling of
dusty potpourri and decorated to within a frilly inch of its
life, but for one night, at the special out-of-season offer of
twenty-five pounds, it's ours.

Last night we went wild and made ourselves cups of tea
from the 'hospitality tray', poured UHT milk from tiny pots,
and took shortcake biscuits from their plastic wrappers for
dunking. After a long bath full of lavender bubbles like in
a magazine, I wrapped myself in the fluffy purple dressing
gown and fell asleep in front of trash TV.

"Morning," says Josh, coming out of the bathroom. He's
wearing the matching purple dressing gown, his giant

hobbit feet rammed into the tiny spa slippers. He takes the calendar off me and beats me to opening the next door. "Mulled wine. Things are looking up at last."

"On a kids' card?"

"Who says it's a kids' card?"

"Duh. The glitter. The polar bears. In knitted scarves."

"Modern kids don't have the patience for this. They can't do delayed gratification like we can. And they want more than plain pictures of a snowman. They want moving images, chocolates, make-up treats."

"If you say so, Grandad."

"Bet you a glass of mulled wine. Budge up."

He flops down on my bed, next to me, rattling the flimsy headboard. "This is the life. Funny how a couple of nights in a cowshed gives you a whole new appreciation for the finer things." He flicks off the slippers dangling from his toes. "Do we have to go today?"

"Yes! Don't be lured by the tiny soaps to stay forever."

"Like that Lotus Casino in the Percy Jackson books. Living out our days dining on room service and wrapped in purple towelling. Sounds good to me." He stretches his arms above his head and sighs deeply. "But seriously, Amber. You don't have to go at all. You can stay with me. My busking can pay for this kind of pad. I reckon we could get that cheap rate again tonight. We're getting by, aren't we?"

I push myself up on one elbow and look down at him.

"You just want me to stay with you, doing what you want to do, eating lotus flowers for eternity."

"No, I don't. Ginger biscuits maybe."

"Stop with the jokes."

I lie back down and stare up at the ceiling and the dusty lampshade. Could I stay with Josh, living on the edges, killing time? Pretending that what happened didn't happen?

"This is going to end at some point, Josh," I say. "Normal life will be resumed. I'll have what I want from the bug-out house, and you'll go back to whatever it is that you do on a daily basis."

"Oh yes. I forgot that we're all going to live happily ever after." He frowns and sits up. "I'm going to go and enjoy my breakfast. You can do what you like." He gets dressed in the bathroom and leaves, without waiting for me.

I flick on the TV while I get dressed because it's better than being in my own head right now. All these conventional lives going on out there. People getting excited about seeing family at Christmas, and what to wear for parties. The smiling morning hosts on the sofas are discussing the best ways to wrap presents. *"But not everyone is going to be having a fantastic festive season, are they, Chris?"* says the woman with the impossibly perfect teeth.

"No, that's right, Zara," he agrees, putting on his serious face. *"Continuing our annual series helping to reunite missing people with their families…"* As I go to switch it off, I freeze,

my finger poised on the remote control. There's a picture of me in my Beechwood uniform from when I joined in Year 12.

"...we're asking for help to trace missing schoolgirl Amber Fitzpatrick. Last seen in the North of England but originally from Somerset, concerns are growing for the seventeen-year-old. There's a number on the screen to call. If you're out there, Amber, please call and let everyone know you're safe."

"And brrr, it's going to be cold out there, Chris."

"Yes, Zara. Let's go over to the weather centre and see if we should all be putting on our bobble hats."

I turn it off and sink down on the bed. If I'm on that TV feature, I'll be on social media. I'll be on missing-person sites. My face getting shared again and again.

I could call Julie. Get her to call off the search party. The pull of home is strong.

Home. I said it. Not a home with parents and all living in a house with a garden and a car on the drive. But somewhere I've felt OK about myself, that supports me to get on, to become somebody different. Somebody better.

Dad gets in the way of all that.

I join Josh for breakfast, chewing slowly through cheap cornflakes from a plastic box while I try to think what I should do.

He packs his bag slowly like I'm making him leave a suite at the Ritz hotel against his will. He keeps commenting on the weather and how bad it is and wouldn't it be better to wait another day. But I'm in a loop of never changing anything if I stay with Josh. He drags it out until check-out time but I finally get him out and walking down the road in the rain towards the tiny town centre.

Josh won't stop talking, he's even worse than usual. He's doing my head in and I can't think properly with all this noise. Eventually, he pulls me out of the rain into a shop doorway. "So, in summary, it's stupid going when the weather's this bad and we've got to do so much on foot and you don't even know exactly where you're going."

Even Josh the loser thinks I'm useless at this, out of my depth. What does he know about anything? I flip.

"Shut up! You're the one slowing me down, Josh," I say, shaking off his hand from my arm. "I had a plan. I should never have let you tag along. Your bright ideas led to all the problems we've had – Mo and Lola's place, slave labour at the hostel, my money getting nicked, those lads, bus roulette. Anyone would think you were trying to stop me from getting up there."

"All those nights I was finding us somewhere safe to sleep, you mean? Shit happens sometimes. I'm not your babysitter. Your option was a bloody cowshed. In this weather. No wonder you got sick. And this mess you're in – it's not down to me."

"The one thing you were right about though is that all this is just hiding from my dad," I say. "Whether it's hiding at school or The Haven or in a field, or, or last night's B&B.

I can't do it forever. I can't, Josh. If I do, he's won. I *am* more kickass than that."

He breathes out deeply. "If you really want to go today, we'll go. Family sticks together."

"We're not family, Josh. You know that, right? Stop pretending we are. You don't have a family, Josh. You've got no one."

He looks crushed but I just can't help myself. I keep on going, pressing all the buttons to hurt him some more. "Your family is a stepdad who liked to beat the stuffing out of you and an alky mother who stood by and let him. Go play Happy Families with them, not me."

I can't bear to see his eyes welling up with tears. He takes a deep breath and pulls his bag over his shoulder.

"Good luck, Amber," he says, so quietly, and heads down the street back the way we came, getting soaked in that stupid green parka with the hood down, never looking back.

As he turns the corner out of sight, I whisper, "Honestly, Josh. I think you're better off without me."

———

I take shelter from the weather and my mood in a quiet outdoors shop and café, looking aimlessly at the overpriced camping gear. I tell myself not to care about the row with Josh, half hoping that a big green parka will come through the door any minute now, still moaning. I buy a drink,

183

thinking it'll give him more time to come and find me. I'll explain to Josh that I was in a foul mood because of the TV appeal, that I'm thinking of chucking it in and calling Julie to stop the search party. I'll tell him that I'm fed up and weary of it all. Weary of being me. Julie said that sometimes asking for help is the strongest, bravest thing to do. Is that true – or is it her usual crap?

I'm not concentrating properly and as I turn from the counter, I knock straight into the young guy standing right behind me. My glass tips, my drink splattering on the floor and down my legs.

"I'm *so* sorry. Completely my fault," he says. He smiles broadly as I dab at my already wet boots and trousers with a disintegrating paper napkin. "I was distracted by the chocolate brownies. Let me get you another drink."

"It's all right," I say. "I'm just going."

"But your drink – and it's hammering down outside. You should wait for it to clear up a bit." He pushes his damp hair off his forehead and grins again. "I'm Will." He holds out his hand with a confidence I'll never have. A confidence that the effortlessly good-looking seem to get for free.

He's expecting me to introduce myself in return but instead I lower my eyes and point to his hiking boots. "Up here walking?"

"Not the best time to be hiking weather-wise, but it's when I could get time off. Always wanted to walk the whole of Hadrian's Wall. Look, I was about to get myself something. Let me get your drink too. I feel terrible."

The woman behind the counter is impatient and tutting. We're attracting attention I don't want. I take the path of least resistance and agree to the drink.

The rain shows no sign of letting up. There's still no Josh. It'll be fine to spend ten minutes here before moving on. I could even ask to borrow this guy's phone to call Julie.

I pick a table in the corner and shake the water off my coat. Will looks two or three years older than me, with an expensive jacket and a body that has plainly spent a lot of time in the gym. As he squeezes on to the old wooden bench opposite me, still smiling and chatty, he's acting like he's known me for ages, not five minutes. I take the glass of fizzy elderflower he offers. "I've put the bottle in the recycling already," he says, like I'm going to criticize his green credentials. "I couldn't decide which cake so I got several. Take your pick."

I nibble at a chocolate brownie, aware of his gaze.

"Let's toast an end to the rain, shall we?" He raises his mug and clinks it against my glass.

Unlike Will, I don't want to talk about the terrible weather or Christmas shopping or the cuteness of the baby who's sitting in the highchair near the counter. I sip my drink while he talks enough for both of us. I can't relax. This was a bad idea.

"I should go…" I start to say.

"You can't rush off and leave me with all these calories to

tackle by myself." He pushes the plate towards me. "Maybe you'd like another drink." He keeps looking at the door. I hadn't thought to ask if he was on his own. For a hiker he's got hardly any stuff – and very clean new boots.

"Where's all your gear – rucksack, waterproofs?"

"In the car," he says.

"I thought you were walking along the wall route," I say, starting to worry that this whole situation is off.

"In stages. Chipping away."

"Where did you start?"

He squirms. "Durham."

"Don't you mean Wallsend? How many days has it taken?"

"What's with the twenty questions?"

He doesn't know. He doesn't know how many days because he hasn't walked it. He doesn't know where it starts! So why would he lie? He isn't smiling any more.

I drain my drink, my hand shaking slightly on the glass, and try to rise but something in my legs doesn't feel quite right. Will slides on to the seat beside me and pushes me back down with an outstretched arm.

"Stay. You need to let yourself recover after that row with the boyfriend."

How did he know about the row with Josh?

He carries on talking about a good walk he did down in Cornwall. About Penzance. Is that where he started walking? Or did he say Newcastle? I'm having trouble following him. He's fading in and out. I shake my head and blink my eyes. Will's gone all blurry. His voice sounds strange now – like a recording that's distorted and slowed down. Are we in Cornwall? Is that what he's saying? What did I want to ask him about? It's important – I think it's important. I'm hot. I pour water into my glass, but it's moving and I spill some on the table. I can't see the café woman. Is she in the kitchen? The only other customer is busy with her baby. I pull at my fleece top. If I could just take it off, I'd feel cooler. But I get in a tangle with my sleeves. He helps me, says we're going for a walk.

I mutter something about how Josh might be coming back, but he says not to worry. He can come on the walk too. It's cooler outside. I'll feel better in the fresh air.

I sway. The room is moving. Things are in my way. Chairs and tables float in and out. Will takes my arm and pushes me towards the exit. I think I might be sick. That would be a bad thing. Maybe it was the cake. Did I have a cake? Can cake make you ill like this? If only I could remember what I'd eaten, I could warn Josh not to touch it. Or what was the drink? Where's the bottle? I pull back towards our table but Will won't let me. Now we're outside. By a car. I don't want to get in a car. Do I? I'm waiting for someone. I can't remember who. It's a misshapen car – the bonnet is bulging and pulsating like a giant heart. That's weird.

"Your car is a giant heart," I try to say but my tongue is swollen and won't do what I want it to do.

He's speaking again. Something about the seat belt, about sitting still like a good girl. About how if only I'd followed the Rules, I'd have been OK.

"Don't you know the Rules?" he says. His hands are strong, pushing me back into the seat. What rules?

"You should have remembered the Rule," he says. *"Trust no one."*

RULE:
PREP FOR THE WORST

Dad became obsessive about his bunker. It wasn't a proper one – it didn't have the levels of reinforced concrete or depth that he wanted. It was just a set of old caves, after all. But he glossed over that in favour of its main selling point: no one knew it was there.

It was secret.

It was just him and me.

Me and him.

I hated the weight of this secret. It bound us together in a way that I didn't want.

He chuntered on about his genes, and blood being thicker than water. But he also talked about obedience and honouring your father and not answering back and that he was the Rules and the Rules were him. I saw only him. All day long. Sometimes through the night too if he decided that our work wasn't done.

His words whirred round and round inside my head. I couldn't get away. I couldn't make it stop.

It was dark.

Dark.

By the entrance, slivers of light came through chinks in the doorway, but we were working further in, within the main chamber, behind a heavy door. There it was pitch-black without the lighting we rigged up.

People often say that, don't they? It was pitch-black. But it seldom is. Usually there's some glimmer from a streetlight or the moon or a phone screen. Somewhere up in the night sky will be the distant flicker of a star. Our eyes adjust, pupils widening, to take in the light. Shapes form and the brain rapidly builds a picture from what it *can* see, filling in the gaps from memory. Your brain pieces together that the ceiling is up, the floor is down, furniture stands on the floor, and so on. But if somewhere is *truly* pitch-black, if no matter how much you try you can see nothing, what then?

I dreaded going in the caves with him to work on our bunker. I had a lamp strapped to my head, like a miner, and the most powerful hand torch we owned. But we were only a failed battery away from complete and utter darkness. We wired up some lighting powered by a solar panel up on the hillside. But it often flickered off without explanation.

And I hated it.

I tried to hide it. But he knew.

He always knew.

———

We built two slatted beds into the main chamber. Bunk beds. Not fun ones with dinosaur decorations and a slide. Ours were more prison-camp style. The mattresses were second-hand with unsavoury stains I didn't like to think about. We draped them in plastic as we hadn't solved the condensation problem in the caves. The stone oozed dampness and salt despite the dehumidifiers that hummed away when we could get the generators working. Dad would freak out from time to time and turn them off, insisting they could be heard from outside, by the government. I mean, what the hell? Sometimes, he preferred to keep watch outside with a set of binoculars, or night-vision goggles he'd wasted his money on.

We installed a water tank and practised purification and filtration methods. It was Wales – we weren't short of rainwater or watercourses. We just had to harness it, store it safely and be prepared for treating it if it was contaminated. I was becoming an expert in water engineering. I even toyed with it as a job. Fantasized that I'd be able to persuade Dad to let me go and train as something that would be useful. Something that would take me away from him.

Because I was getting scared that he would never let me leave that farm.

"What if something happens, what if you can't get back in time?" he said. What he meant was: *What if you don't come back? What if you choose not to come back?*

Because the more time I spent preparing that hellish place for occupation, the more I felt I was digging my own grave.

I thought about my show-and-tell list of SHTF scenarios. I went through the options one by one. And I came to the conclusion that living in that bunker was worse than all the other SHTF scenarios on the list.

I'd rather take my chances with the zombies.

December
15

My head is splitting. The light feels so bright but as my eyes slowly open, I see that no more than a sliver of light is seeping under the edges of the blackout blinds. Striped blinds, blue and white. A kid's room? What kid? It's all too much effort. Thinking hurts. Mum? My head hurts. Why does my head hurt so much? Did I bang my head? I just need to sleep some more.

RULE:
LEAVE NO TRACE

I overheard him talking on his phone that day when Mum left. I heard the word 'Springside' twice.

I was sitting at the top of the stairs, hugging my knees and crying silently. If you ram your fist into your mouth and bite on it, no one can hear your sobs.

I say 'when Mum left' but that suggests she packed a suitcase and walked away. Like going on a holiday or to visit family. We didn't have holidays and we didn't have family or friends to visit.

Not any more.

Or 'when Mum left' could suggest she chose to go, to leave me there with him. To take my chances.

I don't believe she'd ever have done that if she'd had any choice at all.

He took her somewhere. He put her in the car and drove

her and her suitcase to a hospital or a clinic. He wouldn't tell me where. And the only name I had was Springside. That would be enough. It would have to be enough.

After the meltdown. (Meltdown sounded better to me than breakdown.)

Mad.

"Your bloody mad mother."

That's what he shouted at me that day.

Stark staring mad. Raving mad. Mad as a hatter.

Crazy

Nutty

Insane

Loopy

Lunatic

Bonkers

Neurotic

Hysterical

Certifiable

Rule-breaker

Dad was a thesaurus screaming words.

He blamed doctors.

He blamed the council and the government.

He blamed her long-dead parents.

He blamed her.

He blamed me.

He didn't blame himself.

December

16

I'm in a bedroom. I've slept in so many different places lately that I can't remember where I am. The bedding is plain white. The room has nothing but a bed and a chair and my familiar bag. I sit up but my head aches so much I take my time before standing, easing each foot gingerly on to the floor. I'm in a loose cotton T-shirt that reaches my knees. It isn't mine. I shudder to think that someone has undressed me and put me in this. I take in all the details of the room. I don't recognize this place because I haven't seen it before. Someone has brought me here. I try to think back but everything is muddled. I can remember a café, meeting someone. It wasn't Dad. It wasn't Josh. Who?

I step unsteadily towards the door. I pull on the handle, then push. The door's locked from the outside. Now I know I'm in the shit. If I could just shake off this feeling that my whole head is full of cotton wool and think straight... I stagger back towards the window and pull up the blackout blinds. A double-glazed, locked window. No key. The view is of a garden, with a dark forest of spruce trees beyond. No cars, no people. No other buildings. Crows are shrieking in the trees. Dark thoughts cross my mind. I should have called Julie when I had the chance.

Neat piles of my clothes sit beside my bag, laid out in order. Did I do that? They smell of washing powder. I've been here long enough for my kit to be washed. The socks lie in a ball without the boots or shoes. I check the bag. No footwear. The heavy torch has gone, the mini-shovel, the stove, the matches, the snare wire, the fish hooks, the knife, syringes, etc., etc. All the items I could have used to get myself out of here – to *fight* my way out of here – have been removed.

I listen at the door, my ears straining, pressed up against the wood. This place is freakily quiet. Somewhere a clock ticks. Old-fashioned. Maybe it'll chime the hour.

My toiletries bag is by the sink in the small en-suite shower room. I clean my teeth and rinse my mouth. As I wash my face, I begin to feel more like me, more human. How long have I been in this room? My watch has gone. I check in my bag again, going through every pocket. The advent calendar has been left in the bottom – I guess it seemed unimportant. The last day I opened was the fourteenth but I don't know when that was.

I stand at the window, trying to work out the time of day from the grey wintry light. But it's too cloudy. Morning? Late afternoon? I hate that I have no idea. I shower quickly, listening out for anybody coming, and dress in a top and jeans. I feel better for the shower though someone will have heard the water.

I rattle at the door again. This time I shout out. Heavy steps on a wooden, creaking floor approach the room. I stand back, stabilize my weight, get ready for whatever's coming through. For whoever.

The key turns in the lock and a young man in gym gear enters cautiously. He's familiar, if I could just get this fog out of my head. Bill? Will?

"You're awake."

"Obviously."

"I brought you some food." He hands me a bottle of smoothie and a cheese sandwich.

"Is it safe to drink it?" I ask. "You not drugging me today?"

He shrugs his shoulders. "You've been out of it for a while. I may have given you slightly more than necessary. But it's not a precise science and I didn't want you causing a scene."

He shuts and locks the door and leans back against it. "Don't bother thinking about going anywhere. The whole house is secure."

"Where are we? What's the name of this place? Are you

a prepper? Is my—"

"Whoa!" He holds up a hand. "No conversation. Just eat."

I sit on the edge of the bed, slowly chewing bits of sandwich, while he checks my room.

He sees the advent calendar and says, "Two days behind." He opens two doors, humming 'Ding Dong, Merrily on High'. "A present and a snowglobe. How about that? No chocolate." He throws it back in the bag.

The smoothie feels thick and gloopy. I drink the whole bottle but I'm still thirsty and refill the bottle from the tap.

"Thirst can be a side effect, but it'll wear off. Soon have you fighting fit and ready for…"

"For what?"

"I'll leave that as your Christmas surprise. Not my place to ruin it. Shall we go? There's someone who's dying to see you awake."

He leads me along the landing past an old grandfather clock and to a big wooden staircase. The house is sparsely furnished, with dark painted walls. The stairs creak one after the other. My legs don't feel quite right yet, still wobbly, and I grip the handrail in case they fail me.

An American accent booms from a room off the hall. "Amber? Is that you, honey?"

The hairs on my arms prickle and a feeling of dread thumps into my stomach, even though I knew deep down it was coming.

Dad stands up as we enter the room. He's large as life, barely contained victory oozing from his pores.

"Hello, darling. Where've you been?" He leans forwards and kisses my cheek while I stand still as an ice sculpture. "Welcome to our community here at Centurion House. You've already met Will."

All the efforts I made to get here to Centurion House and fate was bringing me anyway. Fate/Will/Dad, whatever.

And now I need to get out.

The room's large with shuttered windows looking on to the garden beyond. A long wooden dining table is covered with papers and boxes, with more piled up around the room. I knew there was an outside chance he'd be storing stuff here now Eden's out of the question. I shouldn't have so easily dismissed the risk that he'd be here too. Stay one step ahead, that's the Rule. Dad takes the chair at the head of the table. Will takes a seat to his side and looks at my dad for instruction.

"You sure are a hard girl to pin down," Dad says. He hasn't broken the smile yet. It's fixed on his face like a mask. He looks well, even up close. He pushes back a chair with his foot and it scrapes on the tiled floor, then he gestures for me to sit with a brief nod of his head.

I'm four, with pee running down my leg, watching him drag Mum by her hair.

I'm eleven with my hands over my ears and my eyes tight shut but I can still hear Mum crying.

I'm thirteen with my arm twisted up my back.

I'm fourteen watching my books burning.

I'm fifteen locked alone in a dark, stinking cave.

I'm all of those people.

Will I ever not be all of those people?

I sit down.

I obey.

Of course.

Honour thy father. *That's the Rule.*

Dad runs his tongue slowly over his lips. He has all the time in the world. He's won.

"Will here has been running around the country, showing your photo at hostels, at bus depots, stations. Up to Edinburgh, a student house in Newcastle. You did well to last so long. But then, I did teach you everything you know."

He's taught me how to lie, how to hide, how to deceive.

"Not in the mood for talking?" says Dad. "No matter. We have plenty of time. We thought we saw you at my event last week. What *was* that ridiculous get-up?" He chuckles.

My mind's racing. He's not meant to be anywhere near here. He must have changed his plans after Josh's stupid stunt with the talk. I should never have gone. I should have trusted my first instincts.

He turns to Will. "You see, Amber and I didn't part on particularly good terms." He lowers his voice, as he uncrosses his legs and leans further towards the younger man, as though he's sharing a confidence. "I'm ashamed to say, we have a few unresolved anger issues in our family, Will. Maybe I'll share it all with you one day in a big show-and-tell." He opens his arms wide.

I dig my nails into my palms to stop myself screaming at him. Does that mean he's got all the Eden Farm records and footage here in this room? Somewhere in all these boxes?

Will looks over at my clenched fists and then back at my dad. "She's got a pretty feisty tongue on her too."

"Ha! That's my girl, a tough cookie," says Dad, bringing his hands together in a loud clap, his eyes flashing. He chews on invisible gum. "We'll have to keep a close eye on her, Will. A very close eye."

He gives me a full minute of silence, waiting in the chair, before asking, "Where did you go when you left Eden Farm? Never even thought about coming back to check on me? And your momma wasn't really well enough, was she? She couldn't look after herself, let alone you."

I breathe in deeply.

He speaks to Will again, "From what I understand, Amber here had to live with strangers provided by the state, instead of living with her own papa." He shakes his head, tutting.

I want to shout that they were *all* better than him, *all* more caring than him. Whether I liked them or not. But I don't. I swallow the words down.

"And then your mother took a load of pills." He tuts.

"Weak. Irresponsible."

Even when she's dead, he can't stop criticizing her.

"It was an accidental overdose," I blurt. This is what I tell myself. She wouldn't have left me voluntarily. She *wouldn't*.

"I wasn't surprised," he says. "Let's face it, she was always more of an overhead than an asset."

His cruelty hangs heavily in the room.

"And what am I? To you?" I ask in a whisper. "Overhead or asset?"

He laughs. "There's that acid tongue again, Will!" He reaches out and places his hands on either side of my face. I tense every muscle but don't move away. I hold his gaze – a small act of defiance.

"Why, you're my flesh and blood," he says. "You're my stake in the future." He drops his hands and leans back in his chair, studying my face. "You're so like me."

He moves forwards again to whisper, "You know it. I know it."

The cold reality seeps into every vein of my body.

Dad slaps his legs and leaps up. "So glad you came to see the talk. I knew your curiosity would get the better of you in the end." He picks up a box from the floor and adds it to the table. "You can help with all this. Bring some order." He pauses. "I just never know when all this could come in handy." He rolls his tongue over his teeth and then smiles. "And there's a big storeroom downstairs that needs better organizing. These preppers up here don't have the discipline of our Rules and systems, honey – though I do appreciate the loan of the place." He looks over at Will. "And we have ourselves a space at the best-equipped bunker facility going. The Ark."

"The supreme covert bug-out spot," says Will, smiling from ear to ear. "We will be so ready for when the shit hits."

"It's the ultimate prepper bunker," Dad says. "Underground, of course, but with access to surface-level polytunnels and a biodome. State. Of. The. Art."

His eyes are blue. I'd forgotten that. I focus on the fleck on his iris and my mind wanders. It's a defence mechanism. I know I should be paying attention to his lies. He's become a salesman selling an overpriced prison cell.

Will eagerly joins in with talk of the selection process, of passing a challenge like he's entered some dystopian competition. I suspect getting hold of *me* was the selection challenge. Are there more disciples like him?

"We need good people like Will here; people with initiative," says Dad. He slaps his minion on the back.

Will stands. "I'll be in the basement if you need me, pressing on with those shelves. I'm going to leave you two to catch up."

Dad nods. "Why, thank you, Will. It's certainly been a while." He turns to me. "A whole new community is building, Amber. People who see the merit in my Rules and understand the need for discipline. You'd be amazed at what people will pay for a place in the Ark."

The Ark. Eden. I'm sensing a theme.

He points over at Will's disappearing back and whispers, "You'd be amazed at what people will *do* for a place in the Ark. So many young people searching for something."

Dad's charmed him somewhere along the line – at one of his talks or in a prepping forum. Will does exactly what he asks without question. In a way that I never could. Will's like the perfect son he never had.

Dad looks at me quizzically. "You don't seem keen, Amber, honey. You never did like being cooped up, did you? But you'll get over it this time. For the greater good." His mouth settles into a firm line. The smile is gone.

In the silence I can hear the distant drip of a tap, the gurgle of water in the pipes.

"Things have changed, Amber. I've changed. You've changed. We all make mistakes. It's what we do afterwards to make up for our mistakes that matters."

I stay silent, glaring.

"I'm somebody now," he adds. "I've learned from the mistakes we – I – made at Eden Farm. That was just an amateur's attempt. It could never have been a long-term solution. Luckily I have funds now. Major funds."

"From where?" I ask. "From people who want to live in your brilliant bunker?"

"Partly. But I have sad news about Grandma too. Her heart." His eyes are cold. I don't believe he shed a tear for her.

"I never stopped hoping I'd find you again. It was always Grandma's fondest wish that we'd all be reunited. Sadly it's come too late for her. But you weren't to know your selfishness would make her sick. Break her heart." He reaches forwards and for an awful moment I think he's going to hug me. He traces my jawline with his finger instead. "You're so grown-up, Amber. A beautiful young woman now."

"I don't want to go to the States, Dad. I want to stay here."

He repeats my phrase in a childish voice. "I don't wanna go to the States, Daddy. I wanna stay here." He leans back again, claps his hands and chuckles. "I knew you were going to say that. I just knew it. That's why I came back to the UK, Amber. I tried setting up something with some folks in Washington State. Turned out they weren't serious preppers. They just wanted a cabin in the woods. A weekend place to sit on the veranda and toast marshmallows. They didn't want to live by the Rules, build a new society. They weren't *serious*. Are you *serious*, Amber? Like Will out there? Like your daddy?" His hand shakes and he tucks it under his thigh on the chair.

We're back to the trick questions. I don't know the correct responses to them. History is repeating itself. Those people in Washington State obviously tired of his stupid ideas. Didn't want to sign up to his Rules. Neither did me and Mum but we had no choice.

"Yes, I'm serious," I say.

"Well, real good to hear it, my little firecracker." He gets up and walks to the window and waits for a moment, like he's weighing up if I'm telling the truth. "I bring good news. The Ark is not in the States, Amber," he says. "It's right here in the good old United Kingdom. Just for you, baby. Just for you."

Rule:
Trust No One

Dad got paranoid about the landline. A few automated calls came through about claiming for an accident or issues with our internet service provider – fraudsters trying to get access to bank accounts or passwords. But he took it as a sign. It was a sign that we were being watched.

The state was watching us, listening in, trying to confuse us when our guard was down. He'd told me so.

The landline had to go.

The state was clever. Dad grew suspicious of the laptop. The state was watching us through the screen. He stuck tape over the camera.

Emails were infiltrating our software, installing spyware. He shut down the laptop. Locked it away.

The postman was an agent of the state. Checking up on us every day. Pretending to be bringing mail when he was secretly taking photographs and planting listening devices. Dad redirected our mail to a post-office box he rented in the nearest town. We had to pick up the mail ourselves. One time he said that the box was under surveillance by a woman in a waxed jacket with a spaniel. We didn't get the post that week.

It was another door to the outside world being shut for me. No phone, no internet, no post.

Dad said the TV was full of lies.

Everything I needed to know, *he* could tell me. Only practical knowledge mattered.

I knew the TV set was on borrowed time. My argument that we needed it to see when the SHTF gave it an extra week or two. But then it was gone. Because smart TVs could watch you in your own home. The state could see what we were doing in our own lounge. On our own sofa. Even if the power was off. We were safest with a basic wind-up radio. No one could trace that or spy on us.

Dad took a hammer to the TV screen one night while I cowered behind the door.

Just to make extra sure.

Dad had systematically removed most reasons for anyone to come to the house. He erected a set of signs round the edge of the property. 'NO TRESPASSING', 'PRIVATE LAND – KEEP OUT'. He added a lock to the five-bar gate. No one could get up the track even if they wanted to.

My world was shrinking

smaller
and
smaller.
Until it was just
me
and
him.
Him
and
me.

But mostly it was him.

I arrange my items on the bathroom shelf and think what I can do with them. My tasks are to find a way to get out of here, and to work out how to overpower ripped Will with a hairbrush, tweezers, a plastic bottle of shower gel and a box of tampons.

Failure is not an option. I can do this. Dad always underestimates what I can do. Preppers adapt to what they have to work with. I smile to myself. They should never have left me the tweezers. There's so much I can do with them beyond plucking my eyebrows.

I try the tweezers in the door lock, twisting them gently from left to right. But it doesn't work. Will has left the key in the other side – which gives me a different idea. The gap beneath the door is tight and I don't know for sure how thick the key is, but it's worth a go. I flatten out the advent calendar card and slide it partially under the door. There's a distant sound of a door closing and footsteps so I wait, holding my breath, until all is silent again, save for the tick of the clock. I poke at the key with the tweezers until it falls from the lock and bounces on the wooden floor. As I carefully pull the card back, it's empty. The key has landed somewhere in the hallway. Damn.

A couple of tiny window flaps have not survived the mission, catching on the rough edge of the carpet. Door three – the snowflake. And yesterday's snowglobe was the other victim. A lonely penguin in a bobble hat trapped in a blizzard. Trapped forever.

I carefully open today's door hoping for something symbolic: a rescue helicopter or a flamethrower? Instead I get a snowman with a carrot for his nose and a stupid grin on his face.

I'm left with squirting the shower gel at them or firing tampons. Maybe the hairbrush. Even I can see the ridiculousness of it all. I try to prise the lid off the toilet cistern thinking I could make a weapon out of a float ball and plastic pipe. But it's fixed solid.

I'll have to try a more subtle approach. My dad is beyond reasoning with. Beyond reason. But Will? I could work on him and appeal to his better nature. Though anyone prepared to slip drugs to a teenage girl might not have a better nature to appeal to. And I'm not renowned for my charm. That's the other major flaw in my plan. But it's worth a go. I pocket the tweezers.

Not for the first time, I think about Josh. Could he have forgiven me for everything I said and gone looking for me? It's not like Josh owes me or genuinely cares about me. It's not like we're really brother and sister. And we're definitely not best friends – he barely knew me a couple of weeks ago. But he's wormed his way into my head somehow. And maybe I'm in his.

He could have reported me missing to the police or social services. Or, most likely, he'll not have contacted anybody in authority at all and is just reading a book and stuffing his face somewhere. I let him down like everyone else in his life. I pushed him away. Why would he help me?

Footsteps approach down the hall. What will they have in store for me today? I'm never left alone in the dining room to do a proper search. Finding extra cash and valuables would be good, of course, but now I know Dad is using this as his base, I'm sure the records from Eden Farm I need are here – if only I can find them. They're worth more to me if I want to move on. Put my side of events.

Yesterday Dad made me go through plans with him, drawing up supply lists. We worked out how much water a community of twenty-five people would consume, how much they'd need for washing and showering, for laundry. He drew up new Rules about how often to wash. I don't know why he bothers with all these categories, sub-clauses, clarifications – whatever he wants to call them. The upshot is that what he says goes. I wash as often as he permits, I eat as often as he permits. In the Ark, the worst thing for me won't be that; it'll be the lack of daylight – though he tells me there are daylight tubes, camouflaged on the surface for security, but permitting daylight to flow down into the Ark. He adds vitamin D supplements to the supplies list to compensate. He rants about the government and the lack of sunlight in Scotland in the winter. Is that where the Ark is? He won't say.

Will unlocks the door. He dangles the key in front of my face and raises an eyebrow. "Been playing with the key, have we? Found it on the floor."

"If you lock up children without any toys, what do you expect? But you can explain all that when the police arrest you for abducting a minor and for false imprisonment. Drugging a child isn't legal either. I'm keeping quite a list on you."

He frowns. "Not this again."

"I want to be there when my social worker gets hold of you," I say. "She will hunt you down for this. You don't know who you're dealing with." I like the image of Julie chucking off her cardigan and rolling up her sleeves to wrestle Will. I half wish it would happen.

"Your father is keeping you here for your own good. Don't you know the Rule: *The ends justify the means*?"

"For my own good? That will sound great at your trial. Tell the judge that *in the real world* and see how it goes."

Will points through the doorway. "Time for breakfast, your ladyship. All laid out in the dining room."

Will thinks that I'm too high and mighty to cook since Dad refused to let me near the kitchen. But aside from all the sharp things locked away in there, Dad and I know better why he's refusing to let me anywhere near his food. On the way downstairs, I ask Will questions about his home, his parents, whether he has any siblings, any little sisters like me? But he shuts it down and changes the subject. Being charming is hard.

"Your father wants you to help with the medical set-up today."

"Aren't you the one who knows all about drugs?"

Will sighs. "We're going to be in the Ark together, Amber. I think we should try to move on and get along. It'll be easier for all concerned."

"You don't think Dad's actually going to let you into his brilliant bunker, do you?" I say, as I pick at the breakfast. "Remember the Rule: *The ends justify the means*. You can't trust a word he's said to you, a single promise he's made. He's using you, Will. If you're so indispensable, why are *you* making toast and *I'm* the one trusted with drawing up water supplies and medical requirements?"

I crunch hard on the toast and chew it slowly and loudly to emphasize my point. So I can't do charming but I can be quite annoying if I put my mind to it. All these years of finding just the right level of sarcasm, tracking down weak spots like a heat-seeking missile. I'm getting under his skin, no matter how hard he's pretending I'm not. The vein on his temple is twitching.

"Actually, Will, where *is* the Ark?" I say in my best little-girl voice, putting on a puzzled face to match. "You know, the one *you*'ve definitely got a VIP spot in. You must have had a full guided tour as you're such a trusted member of the inner circle."

I wonder how many more buttons I can press before Will explodes. His fuming silence tells me something I'd only guessed at – there's no way he's seen the Ark. Dad has no intention of taking Will with us.

His lips move silently. He's counting to ten to control himself. "Your father will be back tonight. You'd better make a start." He points over at the papers at the end of the table.

"Where's he gone today – all day long?" I ask. I look at the size of Will. Can I overpower a trained prepper when the time is right? Or get the keys off that sodding lanyard round his neck?

"Your dad has important people to meet."

"Really? Up here in the countryside? And he didn't invite you along. He likes keeping secrets, the great Mr Fitzpatrick. Want to swap a secret, Will? Like where's he keeping all the valuable stuff? Because here's the thing, Will. Want to know *the thing* about my father?" I whisper the last bit and urge him closer.

Will doesn't take the bait. "*Honour thy father*. That's the Rule."

He slams the door on the way out. And locks it.

I've won a minor skirmish. I got under his skin. But then I remember the war is far from over and the main enemy is my dad. And I'm still locked in a room – just one floor below the one I woke up in. Although this one has tea and toast, and for the first time, I'm on my own in here.

I've made myself so annoying that Will needs a break from babysitting. So maybe I've won more than a minor battle. The front door slams and locks and shortly Will's working off his frustrations on the outdoor gym. He's rigged up a punch-bag off a tree branch and pummels it. I watch him for a moment from the window but then take my chance to go through the boxes of papers, systematically looking for any notes on Eden Farm. Dad was obsessive about noting down all we did. It will be here somewhere. Including, if he's kept it, the footage of the bunker. That's what I need.

I pick through the papers quickly. Sheets of plans, blueprints for the Ark, photos of a sickbay – amazingly equipped – and the beginnings of a list of gear. It's erratically written in his usual spidery handwriting, numbers down one side, pharmaceutical and medical supplies on the other. He certainly needs me to sort it out – it makes no sense. I can't tell what he's already got and what's left to buy.

I check on Will. He's dripping with sweat now and he's

switched to skipping – the rope swishing gracefully from side to side as he works through his routine. He's pushing himself hard. Even Will can't keep that intensity up. How long before he comes back in here? I try another box, and another.

I work through the last pile of boxes, ploughing through seed catalogues, 'How to' guides, a broken set of walkie-talkies I recognize from Eden Farm. He must have just parcelled everything up and put it in storage here while he was back in the US.

Despite all Dad's hints, the records aren't here. Maybe they weren't hints to start with. I've heard what I wanted to hear.

Will is stretching out, lunging and pushing back against the tree trunk. He's winding it up. I'm running out of time.

I grab the final box. As I dig around in its contents I notice something odd about it – there doesn't seem to be as much space inside as its size suggests. When I examine it more closely I find that an extra layer of card has been slotted in to create a false bottom, and there, tucked inside the inch-deep cavity, I find what I'm looking for: SD cards with dates written on them in permanent black marker. These are the records of days in the bunker at Eden. Our underground paradise. These tiny video files hold the miserable evidence of what happened there – and how it ended. All the fuss he made about setting up the system, all the pretence that what he was doing was in some way scientific, evidential, important. I've thought about the power of them all this time, thought about what that final recording could mean for me. Yet here they are, in a mess of old papers, in a cardboard box, in a tip of a room, in a musty house, in the middle of nowhere.

I take them, resealing the cardboard. I check the window but I can't see Will. He must be walking back round. He'll be here in minutes. I shove the three SD cards down the front of my jeans behind the bulky zip and rearrange my jumper. I'll keep them with me now. I've got what I needed. I grab the equipment sheets and sit down with a pen just in time.

Will's back. Red and sweaty. "I'm going for a shower," he says. "I'll be back in five and we can go through the medical supply list together."

I make an elaborate paper aeroplane and draw a pilot in sunglasses sitting in the cockpit. It flies well across the room and drops into the bookcase. The bookcase is empty of course. I wonder how Dad has persuaded his northern contacts to let him use Centurion House. More promised places in the Ark?

I pick up the photo he showed me of the entrance to the Ark yesterday, showing off the blast door that we can shut against intruders. The door is reinforced concrete with a mounted camera and triple-lock system in case the electronics fail. Looks expensive. If he wants to spend Grandma's money on a door to keep out the alien invasion,

I suppose he can. I'd use it to buy a house – far away from him – somewhere on an island. I want a clear blue sea, bright blue sky, set off by a white-painted house with red flowers spilling from window boxes and climbing up the walls, and a green wooden door.

But as my daydream melts back into the image on the photo, I notice that something looks wrong. There's a tiny spiky tree in the background. Half tree, half cactus. A Joshua tree. Pretty sure they don't have those in Scotland. Or anywhere else in the UK.

Wherever his Ark is, it isn't in this country.

He lied.

RULE:
THE ONLY USEFUL KNOWLEDGE IS THE STUFF THAT KEEPS YOU ALIVE

There are many varieties of wild mushrooms.

Some are delicious.

Some can make you sick.

Some can kill you.

It's important to know the difference.

Dad should have remembered that.

We were at Eden Farm. Dad clutched his stomach again and dived for the bathroom. He'd lasted just fifteen minutes between visits this time. The gaps were getting shorter.

I allowed myself to feel some hope as I listened at the door to him vomiting. There was no way he could do the supply run now. But I knew him well enough not to point this out. *He* had to take all decisions. I bit my tongue and waited. I knocked gently at the door.

"You OK, Dad? Can I get you anything? A glass of water?"

He made a garbled noise between retches, which I took to mean 'yes'. My hands shook as I filled the glass, daring to believe that I'd pulled this off. A light, butterflies-in-the-stomach fluttering. I turned the handle on the bathroom door and slowly approached him as he lay sprawled, clutching the toilet bowl. I tried not to focus on the revolting speckles of vomit on his chin and shirt, tried to close my nostrils to the smell. I placed the glass beside him, silently rinsed a facecloth in cold water and wiped the beads of sweat from his forehead.

He threw up again while I patiently waited beside him, my heart in my throat. He wiped his mouth and sipped at the glass of water.

"That's a bit better," he said. He looked terrible. His skin was white with an oily sheen. "But I think I'd best stay here. Could you go on the supply run? It's a long bike ride."

I held my breath. He hadn't let me out alone since Mum had gone.

He retched again. "Collect the post. I'm expecting something from your grandma which I shouldn't let sit in the box."

"I can do it, Daddy."

'Daddy' popped out of my mouth instead of 'Dad'. It was the first time I'd said it in ages. He softened. I was just his little girl trying to help. *Rule: Honour thy father.*

He pulled the keyring from his pocket – the one that never left him – and picked at the small, shiny key for the mailbox and the larger brass one for the padlock on the gate. I tried not to stare, tried hard to play it cool while he was handing me the keys. Handing me my freedom. "Get the list from the kitchen – there's money in the envelope."

"OK. You can rely on me."

I was reliable, trustworthy, dependable. Not the kind to get her mushrooms muddled.

December

18

"Day five in the *Big Brother* house," Will says in a Geordie accent when he unlocks the door this morning. I stare at him blankly. "It was a TV show," he says. "They'd count the days down and film the occupants."

"Were they locked up against their will in a totalitarian regime too?" He doesn't answer. I open the advent calendar to reveal a sleigh, the most impractical form of transport going. Though I'd try anything. Now I've got the SD cards I can think about full-on getting out of here. My only other way out may well be the chimney.

Or Will.

"If only you had some magic flying reindeer to go with your little sleigh," he says.

"Don't think by making some jokes you can get around me, Will. I'm not going to get Stockholm syndrome where

I bond with my kidnapper and sympathize with your cause."

"I'm not a kidnapper and I don't have a cause."

"Yes, you do. You just think you don't. You've adopted my father's cause – which is him over everyone else. Do you think keeping me locked up here is normal behaviour for a loving parent? A couple more days or so and you won't be able to live with yourself. Lima syndrome. Just saying."

"Lima?"

"The more likely outcome in this kidnap situation is Lima syndrome. Where you, the *abductor*…" I articulate every syllable so he knows what he is. "The abductor starts to feel bad for me, the hostage."

"You're not a hostage."

"But I'm not free to go, am I? If it looks like a duck, quacks like a duck…"

He blows a long breath out and his shoulders sag. "Life is simpler if you follow the Rules, Amber." He sounds tired and not at all convinced that his life is simpler for following Dad's Rules.

"My dad is so not the messiah," I say.

"I know that. I'm not stupid. Modern life has got so complicated. It needs shaking up. I want to try something new. Radical."

"Is this some weird gap-year idea that went wrong? Did you think this was going to be better than travelling around Asia or picking fruit in southern Europe? More worthwhile?"

"It wasn't like that. I'd been exploring prepping, reading loads of stuff online and then your dad came and spoke to a group at uni. It clarified things for me." Will perches on the edge of my bed, next to me. "It was, I don't know, like a revelation. There was no point doing a degree, more study, when there might not even be a viable society in a few years' time. Your dad has answers to how we could cope with that."

"I get it, Will. I get how someone with a plan, a passion, can seem like a positive solution. Mum was big on green issues when they first met. She liked all the sustainability side of things, making sensible plans. But then Dad just went further and further. She couldn't cope. She…" I hold my locket tight in my fist.

"I … I'm sorry about what happened to her." Will rests a hand on my arm and squeezes gently. I let him. "I don't know all that went on with your dad in the past but you do still have him. If only you'd give him a chance, listen to his ideas for the future…"

"But *this* isn't about the future or saving the planet, Will. Or being prepared to all live together singing songs round a campfire. This is all about *him*. You've swallowed his whole stinking rulebook. You had a choice about it and you chose this."

I gently rest my head against his shoulder. His arm goes round me and I'm pulled into the warmth of him. His head tilts against the top of mine. His breathing's growing louder. I rest the flat of my palm against his chest, feel his increasing heartbeat. I'm aware of my own too, as my hand moves back and forth across his chest.

"Amber, I…"

My fingers loop around the lanyard.

Will stops, looking down at my hand on the keys, then stands up suddenly, shaking me off. "I should go. I've got jobs to do."

Shit. I've missed my chance. He locks me back in my room. I hammer on the door with both fists. "Look what he's made you do, Will the Abductor. Look what he's made you do!"

RULE:
STAY ONE STEP AHEAD

My heart was beating fast. So fast I worried it would give me away, that Dad would sense it pounding in my chest. I dutifully picked up my Grab-and-Go Bag and flung it casually over my shoulder to hide how much heavier than usual it was.

I pulled out the bike and trailer from the woodstore, stowed my bag and cycled off down the lane, dodging the potholes, not minding the gathering clouds on the horizon. Keep on peddling. That's all I had to do. It was over. I hadn't been beyond the gates of Eden Farm on my own for weeks.

Every revolution of the bike wheels took me further away from *him*.

Stay one step ahead. That was the Rule. And I had thought ahead, worked through my plans and what could go wrong.

Strategized.

I had his cash in my pocket. And my own items of jewellery stashed in my bra. Dad was always banging on about how when the collapse of the monetary system came, gold and jewellery would have more value than banknotes.

I reckoned I had at least three hours before Dad realized I was late back. He was probably too busy throwing up to even notice what time I'd left. That could buy me another hour.

If I didn't come back, he'd think at first that the bike had a puncture. He'd be looking for a sensible reason that his dutiful daughter had let him down. *Rule: Honour thy father*.

Meanwhile I would get back to civilization and doctors and phones and computers. I would go through every place called Springside until I found Mum. And then we would run.

I'd followed the Rule: *Stay one step ahead.*

I was free.

Dad's back. He is free to come and go as he wishes while I'm locked up in Centurion House, hour after hour, day after day, supervised by Will. Wherever he's been, he's back with new enthusiasm – more lists and more choices to be made. We spend the morning in the basement storeroom finishing reordering the shelves of supplies to his precise requirements. *Everything has its place.*

Dad escorts me back to the main room to assign me another task. I offer to go through catalogues for gas and chemical-attack masks to see if we should replace the ones I selected from the basement store and stored safely in my Grab-and-Go Bag. Other teenagers are probably browsing online gift stores, choosing novelty Christmas presents, and I'm weighing up the specifications of air-supply respirators versus filter masks. Merry Christmas, me! I take ages over it until I know the mask I have is perfect, and laboriously record my findings on his stupid spreadsheets so that he doesn't give me something else to do.

The calendar today has a perky little robin. My mum collected robins. After she died, I went through her belongings, with Julie getting in the way and being all melodramatic about it. All those robins I'd given her, saved up my money for over the years, and one I'd nicked from a charity shop, somehow three of them survived all the turmoil and the moves. But I didn't want them back. They reminded me that nothing I'd done had helped her. What use was a cheap pottery robin? There's no use looking back. None at all.

But still, today, I stare at the little bird picture and remember the ones I threw away. What would Mum make of this? Despite our efforts, Dad's won. He has me back, at his beck and call. A caged bird.

Dad paces around, glares at Will through the window and raps at the glass for him to cut his session short.

"I can't decide between stainless steel and plastic water drums," says Dad, agitated. "So many different views on which one."

"Do you want me to look online?" I offer, thinking there *must* be a smartphone or a laptop here somewhere. He's trusting me more. Today my watch and some more contents of my Grab-and-Go Bag were returned. The ones you can't use as weapons.

"I've got the latest info here," he says, handing me a set of research papers.

"Shall I look for any others?" I persist.

He tuts and shakes his head. "Amber – you know the Rule. *I* give you what you need to know. There's no internet here. That's not allowed."

Except for him, apparently. One rule for him, one rule for everyone else.

I leaf through the papers, trying to care whether there's more bacteria in water that's stored in plastic or stainless steel but really just needing to look busy so he doesn't give me something worse to do. He's made random jottings in the margins, exclamation marks. He flits from one thing to another, not taking decisions on anything.

"The internet is full of lies and the government will track what you do on there," he says suddenly. "Do you *know* how damned easy it is to trace someone by the trail they leave?"

He holds his pen in mid-air, eyebrows raised. It's not a rhetorical question, he wants an answer.

The picture of Neville the vicar in the newspaper passes through my head. Is Dad hinting that he's responsible for that?

"I do know, yes," I say quietly.

Satisfied, a smug smile playing on his lips, he returns to the mountains of paper.

Milky winter sunshine falls through the window, making patterns on the wooden floor.

"I haven't been outside for days," I say, ready to play on his current feeling of triumph. "And we've been doing this for hours. Can I get some fresh air? Some vitamin D."

He purses his lips.

I swallow down the last of my self-respect. "Please, Daddy."

He leaves the room and I worry that I've pushed it too far, blown my chance to take a look outside, but he returns and silently passes me my boots. It feels strange to put on footwear again after all these days shut up in here. Strange but liberating.

He takes my hand and leads me to the front door, using his key to unlock it.

I revel in the rush of cold air and the sun on my face as we stand on the doorstep, then he leads me like a pony round the house. The gravel drive winds away out of sight into the trees. A car's tucked by the side of the house under a camo tarpaulin. An old prepper trick, so that no one with binoculars can see the metal car glinting.

The trees my room look out on stretch away up the hillside towards what must be Kielder Forest. A paddock sits on the east side with overgrown grass and a rundown barn in the far corner. I can't see a single other building, a road, a pylon, or a phone wire. Nothing. As expected, no one is nearby. I hear only wind in the trees, and birdsong. This place is perfect for preppers. Too soon my tour is over, and we're back at the main door. Back to being locked up.

A plane's overhead, way up in the crisp blue sky, leaving white fluffy trails behind it. People going on business trips or holidays. I raise my head to watch – and wish I was up there. Dad follows my gaze then grabs my arm roughly and pulls me back inside.

"It can't see us, Dad," I say.

"It's the chemtrail," he says, breathlessly. "They don't want you to know, but they spray us with chemical agents. All the time."

I'm struggling to understand what he means. He's talking nonsense again, like someone who's had a bump on the head. But he's so intense, his hand gripping my arm so tightly it hurts. "You mean the white trails? I thought they were condensation trails," I say.

He laughs. A sudden cackle that echoes in the empty hall. "That's exactly what they want you to think, stupid. That's what they tell you in their books. They lie, honey. *We* know the truth. We have to protect ourselves, Amber."

Dad's always trodden a fine line between reasonable fear and irrational conspiracy. The sensible precautions anyone should take versus full-on fortified ex-missile silo to sit out the century. What tips someone from the rational to the irrational?

He puts on a front. He pretends. He cons people like Will. But not me. I know him. And I know he's getting worse.

RULE:
NEVER BREAK THE RULES

The receptionist at the doctors' surgery didn't like:
   rain dripping off my jacket on to the carpet
   bikes leaning against the glass porch
   girls who don't give their name
   drumming fingers on the desk
   bad manners
   swearing
   me.

I was out of practice at asking for help.

As I stood in the rain, trying to wipe the saddle dry, a young woman came out, sheltering under the porch to have a cigarette.

"You showed her, like," she said. "She can be a right stuck-up cow, that receptionist. Best entertainment I've seen all month, that was."

She offered me a cigarette. My hands shook as I lit it from hers, still fuming about the argument. I coughed as I breathed in.

"Asking about Springside?" she asked.

I nodded, spluttering.

She took a slow, long draw on her cigarette, her thin face becoming even thinner.

"It's the new name for the mental health unit just near Swansea. My cousin was there for a while – post-natal depression. Think they thought a name like Springside would pep it up, make it sound like a hotel."

"Where exactly?"

"On the station road beyond the massive Tesco and the leisure centre. I visited her." She reached over and squeezed my arm. "It was nicer than I thought it would be. And my cousin got sorted – home with her kids in a few months. Know someone there, do you?"

"I … I'm not sure. Maybe."

"She'll be looked after there, love."

She threw her stub on the ground and put it out with a grind of her shoe into the wet grass. "Better get back inside before that bloody woman gives my appointment to someone else. Be all right?"

I nodded, wafting smoke from the cigarette I was happier keeping away from my mouth. I couldn't speak, couldn't say thank you because I couldn't trust my voice not to crack. I couldn't let myself cry, deep stupid sobs that would take my bravery away.

I knew where Springside was.

———

Next stop was to check the post. I'd hoped for a letter from Mum but instead I found a money draft from Grandma and more prepping literature.

I had a plan now: train to Swansea, get Mum. Dad didn't like anywhere with CCTV so I hadn't been on a train for ages. He didn't want the state logging his movements and recording his face. MI5 obviously had nothing better to do than watch live coverage of who's on the platform at a small station in Wales. Maybe if I had been anywhere near a station in the last three years, I'd have known that on some trains you have to book the bike in advance. I argued this point at the barriers, hastily detaching the trailer to make the bike smaller, looking at the near-empty train pull into and leave the platform. Without me.

The next train was four hours later.

New plan. This was fine, I told myself. Regroup. It was about thirty miles by road. I'd cycle to Swansea, collect Mum and then we'd get away together. London, Scotland, France. Somewhere. We'd manage.

My hood flew back as I pedalled but I didn't care. The rain was getting worse. Great pools of water formed on the roads. The bag was pulling on my back and knocking me off balance. I wished I'd brought the trailer after all, rather than leaving it at the station bike rack. I thought I'd be less conspicuous on the road without it but what if Dad came looking and found it? He'd assume I'd got the train and that narrowed down my possible destinations – including Swansea. I should have hidden it. I should have thought ahead. I'd made a mistake.

I'd broken a Rule. *Stay one step ahead.*

It would take me hours still to get to Springside. I counted through the minutes, counted through the Rules.

Never break the Rules

It was OK to have broken one.

It was OK to have broken one.

It was OK to…

I rounded the bend and skidded to a halt, my brakes squeaking. A van was blocking the road, parked across both sides of the carriageway: a white flatbed truck with a cracked nearside headlight that I recognized only too well.

"Get lost, did you?" Dad stood by the truck, leaning against the side of it, his arm stretching across the roof. He was pale. He retched and spat on the ground. His stomach must have thrown up all it could.

My dad – full of bile.

He walked towards me. "You've been gone a long time."

"It was a longer ride than I thought. I'm out of practice. I got a puncture on the trailer too. I had to leave it. By the station."

I spoke too quickly. My breath was shallow. I sounded guilty. The station wasn't by the post office. Or the pharmacy. And the tyres didn't have a puncture.

"And the storm came in," he said. "I was worried."

"Just a bit of rain," I said, as the drops ran down my face. They blurred my vision. "I'll cycle back." I gripped the handlebars. We both knew I was facing the wrong way to cycle home.

He shook his head. "Get in." He said it so quietly that I thought I'd misheard him. "Get. In." He opened the passenger door wide. Rain pummelled the seat while I stood there, holding on to the bike so hard my knuckles were white.

"But the bike…" I started to say, but he grabbed my arm and pulled me off it. The heavy bag on my back sent me even more off balance and I fell to the ground, scraping my leg on the pedals. He dragged me and the bag towards the truck, shoved me into the front seat and slammed the door. I reached for the door handle, but the click of the lock sounded. He glared in at me through the window. I stared back at him, like a game of blink. He broke our locked gaze first.

For a moment I felt victorious. I'd beaten him. But I hadn't, had I?

I shouldn't have broken a Rule. *Never break the Rules.*

He lifted the bike and threw it in the back of the truck.

December

20

An alarm sounds in the hallway. Will looks up, surprised. We've got used to the monastic silence – no radios, no TVs, no music – so the sudden beeping makes us jump. "It's the perimeter alarm," he says. "Anyone coming to join us yet?"

Dad looks puzzled and shakes his head. "What day is it?"

I point over at my advent calendar propped up in the hallway. "The reindeer says it's the twentieth," I say. "Too early for Santa."

Will tuts at my sarcasm but rises. "I should check it out. Probably just deer. The forests are full of them." But before he gets to the hall, there's a knock at the front door. Dad bundles me into the dining room, one arm up my back, one hand firmly over my mouth. It's the first time he's touched me since he kissed me when I got here. That was bad enough but this, *this* triggers something in me. The fear's back.

I recite the Rules in my head. That's how stupid I am. Using the very thing that's made me like this. I try to substitute new Rules. *Rule number one: Don't put up with this. Rule number two: You can change the situation. Rule number three: Survive.*

Then, a faint voice in the hall – Josh's voice.

"All right, mate. Sorry to disturb you. Just looking for a friend of mine. Amber Fitzpatrick. Beautiful girl, long brownish hair, funny?" He pauses. "Kind of annoying."

"Sorry. No. Never heard of her," says Will. "It's just me and my family up here on holiday. Why would your friend be here?"

"Just a theory. The place meant something to her. If I leave you this number – could you call it if she turns up?"

"Sure. I'll show you out."

"People are trying to find her. Her picture's all over the media," says Josh. "Social workers, vicars, me. The police."

"I'll keep an eye out. How did you get through the gate, by the way?"

"I jumped it. Snagged my favourite trousers – that barbed wire is vicious for a holiday cottage. You should get a doorbell. How do you get your pizza delivered?" His voice is fading and the front door pulls shut with a thud. Will must be walking him along the gravel drive back towards the gate.

Dad tightens his grip across my mouth. A feeling courses through my body like electricity. What is it? Hope? Rebellion? Josh is a link to the outside world. People are looking for me. This is going to end, one way or another.

I drive my elbow into Dad's stomach and twist my body to force all my weight against him. I don't manage to throw him in one movement but he's off balance for a second and I use the moment to get out of his grasp and dash to the door and scream out, "Josh!" Pain surges through my leg as Dad lunges for my knee and pulls me down. I slam my wrist on the hard floor and the breath is knocked out of me. He crawls over my legs and pins down my hands by my side, my face rammed into the floor. The tweezers, still in my pocket, are digging into my hip.

"Shut your mouth," he hisses at me.

My hand is by my pocket. I wriggle my fingers and slowly, slowly pull out the tweezers, calculating if I can reach up to his face, his blue eyes, before he blocks me.

"He's gone," he says. As he relaxes his grip, I twist and plunge the tweezers into his thigh. They're not sharp enough, they don't even pierce his jeans. A mosquito bite on a lion.

They annoy him.

I annoy him.

And I will pay the price.

Will's back, boldly striding into the room. "It was the druggie dropout Amber was hanging around with before I picked her up. He's clueless. But he…" He stops mid-sentence.

From my position on the floor with my father wrestling my arms behind me, red-faced and furious, I can see how Will's expression changes.

Dad pulls back. He stands up and dusts himself off, while I scramble backwards and rest against the wall, my knees pulled up. I don't want either of them to see me shaking. My kneecap throbs where it hit the floor. Fighting with Dad isn't going to get me out of here.

"Mr Fitzpatrick," says Will, stuttering. "I-I don't think that's the way to treat Amber."

He's calling me 'Amber', seeing me as a person.

"She was jeopardizing everything."

"I walked him to the gate. He's gone." He pauses and says hesitantly, "You, you can't keep someone against her will like this. It's not right."

Dad smooths down his hair. "*The ends justify the means.* This is for her own good."

"It doesn't look like that to me."

"I'm building something bigger than you. The Rules…"

"The Rules are meant to be something good to live by."

Dad's anger is building again. Will takes his silence as permission to continue criticizing him, disrespecting him. He doesn't understand that with Dad the silence is more terrifying.

"And what if the police come next? What will the others in the Ark think? How will the Rules work?"

"*I am the Rules and the Rules are me,*" spits Dad.

I stand hesitantly and ask for some water. The shakes have stopped. Who would win in a full-on fight between Dad and Will? Will surely. He's younger and fitter. How soon before it comes to that? The hold Dad's had on him is failing. How can Dad look like a hero when he's wrestling his daughter on the floor?

"That's enough, Will. I'm very disappointed in your operational security," says Dad. "No one should be able to walk right up to the door like that. Bring forward the timeline for setting up the electric fencing. Review the op-sec now."

"But shouldn't we check with the prepping group. It's their…"

"Sort out some better fencing," says Dad, holding up his hand to interrupt him. "Now. Take the car. And if you want to take your place beside me in the Ark, don't question how I run my family affairs."

Will looks over at me. "Is … is she going to be OK?"

"Of course," says Dad. "If she follows the Rules."

Will leaves me with him. I thought he was wavering, rediscovering his sense of right and wrong. But it'll take more time. I've exposed a chink. I just need to keep picking away at it.

Dad turns back to me. He's smiling again, which freaks

me out. "The electric fencing will also help with the electromagnetic fields from the mobile-phone masts. They think they can poison us but we know better."

That makes no sense at all but he appears to believe it.

"They?" I ask, though I can guess the answer.

"The government, of course. Not just here. They all work together – the deep state trying to keep us subdued with electrosensitivity."

There's no trace of the anger from earlier – it's like a switch flipped and the last half hour hasn't happened. As though he's explaining something to a schoolchild. There's something wrong with how his brain works, I swear. I ease myself up, rubbing my knee, and edge slowly towards the door. He's rearranging the paperwork that fell to the floor in the scuffle, humming to himself. A tear rolls down my cheek, despite myself. I don't know if Josh was telling the truth or bluffing. Either way, he's gone and I'm trapped in Dad's unpredictable world again. Constantly on the alert for fight or flight. Am I ever going to get out of here?

He turns and I think he's about to launch himself at me again to keep me from the door. But instead he smiles an even bigger smile and says, "Don't worry, Amber. Blood's thicker than water. If it's a choice between taking you and taking Will, I choose you, baby."

He picks up the tweezers as though he's never seen them before and puts them on the table. Sweat patches are visible on his shirt from our tussles, his face still red. I follow him into the hall. He picks up the advent calendar, studying the tiny doors. "Four more days," he says.

"I didn't think we'd be celebrating Christmas. Nothing's ready," I say. "I didn't get you a present yet."

He shakes his head, smiling, and beckons me back into the room before closing the door behind us, as though he doesn't want anyone to hear. Even though Will's out of the house.

"It's already here, Amber." Something wild flickers across his face. "We've all been waiting for the *one* thing. The one scenario. The one SHTF episode. But I've come to realize it's already here." His voice has dropped to a whisper. He pats the chair next to him and I sit down, knees together, back stiffly upright, on tenterhooks.

"Climate change, political upheaval, betrayers of democracy, rising violent crime, civic unrest. All around us. Everywhere you look." He thumps his fist on the table. "We're in denial. Modern society is already imploding. It's already here." He crouches beside me and places his hands on my knees. I freeze. "It's already here, baby girl."

He strides across to his boxes and pulls out the plans and photos of the Ark. "Luckily we've got a survival option. I've been blessed to have gotten the funding, the knowledge and the infrastructure. All you and I have been doing is the final tweaks to an amazing project. As good as anything in the States today. Better than that. The Ark is the best bug-out place on earth."

He arranges the papers proudly on the table and pulls me over to look.

"We'll be a new society, living by the Rules, able to defend ourselves if trouble comes knocking." He's speaking so quickly, he pauses to wipe saliva from his lips. He can't keep up with himself. "I can prove all the systems work. Run a proper stress test this time. Show them we can do it. Go for full implementation."

I tense up at his mention of the stress test. I've done one of those before and it didn't end well.

"I'm your only chance to survive, Amber. Don't you see? We're going for a lockdown. Four days' time. Christmas Eve."

RULE:
SURVIVAL IS EVERYTHING

I thought I'd got good at lying, at disguising the common signs.

But truth and lies were irrelevant. By this stage, whatever I said was wrong.

I couldn't explain what had happened

why I'd left the trailer at the station

why I didn't have the shopping

why I was cycling on a back road away from the town, away from Eden Farm

why he was so sick after the lunch I made

and I wasn't sick at all.

The journey back felt like a narrowing of my life. Other people in cars dropped away. Hints of normal lives happening in normal houses – a kid splashing in puddles in his front garden, a couple walking a border terrier, a colourful trio of cyclists on the lanes. We left them all behind and we were left with nothing more than our narrow world.

Dad's world.

An escape plan in reverse. A gate closed and locked again. This time Dad added another padlock.

The never-ending lane to our property. The hedges high above us on both sides, sometimes curling over the top, straining to make a tunnel. And all the time on that lane, he was silent. He didn't need to ask me to explain myself any more.

He knew.

He knew.

He knew.

He pulled over a couple of times to retch. His whole body convulsing.

Another gate. Another lock.

At the house, I walked in ahead of him. He made me strip to my underwear. He went through my pockets and took back the cash. He saw the lumps in my bra and made me hand over the jewellery. He threw my damp clothes back at me and I turned away embarrassed and pulled them back on. I moved towards the stairs and my bedroom, hoping this was over.

"Your Grab-and-Go Bag is by the door."

I had a glimmer of hope that he was chucking me out.

I even thought about the next train to Swansea.

But they say: it's always the hope that kills you.

He had something else in mind entirely.

"Scenarios can arise at any time," he said.

No, no, no. Not that.

He pulled on a jacket and handed one to me.

"Pick up your bag," he said calmly.

He was scarier when he was calm than when he was screaming.

I hung back.

He reached into the hall cupboard. I knew what he kept in there.

He pulled out the shotgun.

"I sure hope you're not going to take advantage of my sickness to run away again, Amber."

I swallowed. I shook my head. He wiped his sweaty forehead with a shaky hand.

The fever was making him worse.

"Dad," I started to plead, but he placed a finger on his lips.

"No more talking. Shush." The shushing came out as an angry hiss, spittle landing on my sleeve.

"But—" I didn't finish because he slapped me across the face. The way I'd seen him do to Mum. I instinctively grabbed at his arm to resist, but he flipped my hand and bent my arm up my back, pushing me against the wall. His classic, practised manoeuvre. Even sick, he was too strong for me. I flailed with my other arm, knocking a picture to the floor, cracking the glass.

"*I am the Rules and the Rules are me*," he whispered in my ear. "What are the Rules?"

He applied more pressure to my arm and my cheek was pressed further against the wall. I squeezed the words out. "*Rule: Trust no one. Rule: Prep for the worst. Rule: Honour thy father.*"

I recited them on a loop out of the house, carrying my bag. He walked behind me with a half-cocked shotgun, a faded baseball cap on to shield him from the rain, like he'd stumbled out of a movie. I just needed the sheriff or a superhero to come and stop it.

No one came.

I was drenched but I barely cared. It seemed appropriate. The world was stormy, raging, weeping. As if it shared the terror I didn't dare to show.

That's the thing. Keep your own thoughts. He could make disjointed words come out of my mouth as we slipped our way up through the woods and hillside. "*Rule: Never break the Rules. Rule: Everything has its place. Cans and jars should face forwards and be exactly one centimetre apart. Sets of clothes should be laid out in order, ready to put on in an emergency. Cutlery must be perfectly straight at right angles to the edge of the table. Glasses must be a fist's distance forty-five degrees from the edge of the knife.*"

But inside, deep down, so deep that sometimes I'd feared she'd gone and left me too, there was still Amber.

Me.

I was in there.

Somewhere.

And I was screaming back at him.

———

When we reached the bunker, I figured he was going to make me spend the night there. As punishment. Petty, petty punishment for my unspoken crimes.

"Rule: Kill or be killed. Rule: Survival is everything."

But he was rambling on about stress testing, about how I could redeem myself by testing it for him. Prove myself.

Save myself.

He took out his notebook and pretended this was a rational, scientific way of behaving.

He switched on the video camera as though this was proper research rather than locking me in a stinking, dark cave. For punishment.

I was calculating, thinking twelve hours, twenty-four hours maximum. That's how long they run stress tests for. I could do it. I could sleep for most of it, eyes tight shut. I'd spent whole days in there before, working on the place.

Now I was inside, I shivered. My clothes were still damp. The temperature in the bunker was a steady eleven degrees. Perfect for storing cheese or wine. Not people.

It gets in your head, being locked up like that.

It changes you.

Forever.

December
21

Dad's been even touchier than usual today. He questions me about Josh. About how he knew to look for me in this area. Who does he work for? What's his real name? Dad's had all night to build a huge web of conspiracy theories.

I lie. Unconvincingly.

He steps up a gear late afternoon, talking about intruders, spies, the need to defend ourselves. He does an inspection of Will's hastily deployed electric fencing and isn't impressed. His disappointment with the site's op-sec is gone over and over, like yesterday. He can't let it go. Will's electric fencing is for stopping livestock roaming – not humans. Dad wants it modified to make it stronger. First light tomorrow, he wants Will back on it. A ring of steel. Even Will, the disciple, is looking uneasy, as Dad cleans his hunting rifle and dons his full-on prepper-in-the-woods outfit.

"Survival is everything, folks," he says, adding rounds of ammunition to his utility jacket pockets. "*Kill or be killed. That's the Rule. If that hippy hobo comes back, I'm ready for him.*"

"Now, hang on a minute, Mr Fitzpatrick," says Will. "He's harmless."

Dad's blue eyes fix on me and a chill runs down my spine. "That's just where an attack can come from. Someone you believe to be harmless. *Stay one step ahead.* That's the Rule."

"And what if you decide tomorrow that I'm a threat?" says Will. "Or Amber. Or the other preppers joining us. Do we get exiled beyond the electric fence, beyond the wall?"

Will then makes the mistake of mentioning what's legal in *this* country rather than in the backwoods of Ohio. There's no point using reason with Dad. That makes things worse, not better. I leave Will to learn that for himself. The hard way.

I back slowly out of the room as they argue. "I'm going to check the food store," I say. "To make sure everything is in its place." But no one hears.

He's already made me put everything in its place. The cans and jars are now facing forwards, one centimetre apart. I know exactly what's there if I need to use it. I'm beginning to think just running away from Dad isn't going to solve anything. It's gone too far for that. It'll never be over with him. I'm going to have to play this a whole new way.

I turn the key, flick on the lights, go down the steps and feel an uncharacteristic cold breeze in the usually stuffy room. There's a scuffling noise and I grab the broom, ready to do battle with a harvest mouse or rat again.

The windows are small and high and I can't reach them, but I can see that one of them has been forced from the outside, splintering the wooden frame. The culprit's not a mouse. Behind the last shelving stack is a heap of green coat and gangly limbs, eating a can of sardines with his fingers: Josh.

"Finally!" he says through a mouth full of fish, oil running down his chin. "I thought you'd never come. Are you all right? I've cut my arm and knackered my ankle from breaking through that stupidly small window. It's low on the outside but then there's a massive drop in here."

I hug him instantly.

"If they've laid a finger on you…" he says.

"I'm all right, honestly. But Josh, they mustn't know you're here. Dad's gone nuts since you came." I gather the contents of the first-aid box he's managed to scatter around him, and the opened bottle of whisky.

"Ha! I'm not stupid. I got that impression yesterday when the gym bunny marched me back to the gate. I waited until he drove off later before I tackled the obstacle course of getting back in. Why do you think I haven't shouted for help?"

I'm touched that he's come looking for me but his arrival – in this state – has complicated my life somewhat. I help him to a chair in the furthest corner of the basement, well hidden by the last racks of equipment.

"I can tell when someone's lying, Amber. It's my special talent. That and buses." He smirks. "Said I was Sherlock Holmes and you were Watson, didn't I?" He taps his head. "My BS monitor was on full alert. *And* I saw your advent calendar on the hall shelf. I'd recognize those polar bears in scarves anywhere."

"This is all very sweet," I say. "But Sherlock Homes didn't 'rescue' people by knackering his ankle and getting locked up with them – did he?"

"Aha. You'll remember I also said that terrible life choices were my speciality."

"No shit, Sherlock."

"I was mightily hacked off with you after the B&B. I went to visit Rev Neville. He looked terrible. On the plus side he's had a constant stream of lady visitors bringing him casseroles and bottles of wine. I helped him clear the backlog. But I got to thinking, what sort of a sort-of brother would I be if I ran off when the going got tough? You and I, Amber, we both push people away. We can be so bloody difficult that people don't want to help us. Because, and here's the important thing, we fear rejection. Deep, huh? Ow! That stings."

I tackle the cuts on his arm. He's had a go himself but

I reapply antiseptic and steri-strips and dress it properly. While Josh, being Josh, tells me his entire recent life story since our argument, in whispers. He wants to start at the beginning and tell it all. He can't jump through to an executive summary. He wants me to hear all his cleverness. He still doesn't get that this is not a game. The clock is ticking and Dad's walking around upstairs with a rifle.

"It's wild up here. There's no mobile signal, no big shops, haven't even seen a petrol station yet. Hardly any houses," he says. "Though that's a good thing as I've been traipsing about the district, phoning in to Neville when I can. He's been plotting the search on a map from his sickbed like GCHQ and telling me where to try next. He's loving it. Speeded up his recovery no end. We have given meaning to his dull existence."

I interrupt his flow. "I need to get back upstairs, Josh, before I'm missed."

"We had a method. Neville has all these contacts in the local history society or something. Turns out Centurion House is a pretty common name up here because of the Romans and Hadrian's Wall and all that. We drew up a shortlist of possibles near the reservoir. I look at a house, suss it out, speak to any occupants, rule it out and move on," he says. "I was suspicious of this place because it had so little happening, and I saw a light before a blind was rolled down. Blackout blinds. I remember you said they were a real prepper thing so you don't give away that anyone's living there when the zombies are roaming the district or whatever. And all that over-the-top security at the gate."

"And all this time, I thought you never listened to me."

"I listened. I just didn't take it seriously."

I put a gas lantern and a pile of food around him and place a bucket nearer for peeing in. "Blimey, you think of everything," he says. "That makes you my favourite kind of prepper. I slept in a stable the other night, like baby Jesus. Except my stable stank of horses and no one brought me any presents. Ow!" He flinches again as I examine his ankle.

"I think it's sprained, not broken. But without an X-ray..." I bandage it for support.

"I've been self-medicating with the booze, to be honest. Whisky seems to work better than the paracetamol."

"Dad's getting crazier. If he finds you here, he'll really hurt you – you'll forget all about the pain in your ankle. I'll do my best to stop anyone coming down here."

He clocks the bruises on my wrists from yesterday.

"Shit, Amber. Now I see why you preppers need to know first aid – you're always beating the bejesus out of each other."

"Things are kicking off between Will and Dad. Just stay here and don't make a single noise." I give him some strong painkillers. "Take these. Sleep off your medicinal hangover."

"Don't worry, I can't even stand by myself, let alone

manage all those steps. Prepared. Shit scared. When are you coming back?"

"When it's safe for you. And for me. At least Neville knows you've found me."

Josh clears his throat. "No, not exactly. I wanted to definitely see you before I called in the cavalry."

"OK. You've seen me. Have you called him?"

He pulls out his phone from his pocket and waves it. "No signal. I'm nearly out of charge too. There's a phone box about three miles away. I left my gear in a hedge right by it. Though that won't be so easy now…" He looks down at his ankle. "I guess there's no landline?"

I raise my eyebrows. "Jeez. I never thought of that, Sherlock," I say. "Of course there isn't."

"The Rev does have an action plan to call the police if he doesn't hear from me by eight tomorrow morning. He insisted. What's *your* Plan B? Smoke signals?"

"Amber?" Dad's angry voice echoes through the house. My stomach twists.

Josh grimaces through a flinch of pain. "What are you going to do, Amber Warning? Nothing dangerous. I'm kind of fond of you."

"I'm kind of fond of you too. We're practically siblings, remember. The great unwanted ones. I'm working on Will. I have a Plan B and C brewing. I'm waiting for my moment when…"

"When the SHTF?"

"Something like that." I run back up the stairs. "Coming, Dad!" I shut the door behind me, locking it, and put the key in my pocket.

Will pushes past me in the hall, muttering under his breath, and goes upstairs, taking the steps two at a time. "He's effing lost it! His Rules are completely out there!"

Dad's walking the hall – a bundle of frustration and rage, clenching and unclenching his fists. "I'm going to check the perimeter," he says. "Myself. Do the job properly."

'Perimeter', as though we're in an army camp. As though we're at war. Maybe we are. He secures the front door after himself, leaving me a prisoner still. I hope he concentrates on his beloved electric fencing and doesn't notice the smashed-up basement window in the dark.

Will's thudding about upstairs. Their argument was a bad one. Is this the endgame? All this anger. All this noise. Stress. Pressure. I sit on the bottom step with my head in my hands just wanting it all to stop, to go away forever. A man in a dog collar in a vicarage miles away holds the power to call the police at eight. That's about twelve hours before anyone comes and sees what Dad is like. A lot can happen in that time.

When Will finally appears, red-faced and tight-lipped, he's carrying two large bags. I move out of the way and he places them by the mat. "Where is he?" he asks.

I jerk my head towards the door. "Inspecting the fence again, looking for the hordes of invaders."

Will tuts and shakes his head. "Look, Amber. You should know that…"

I hold up my hand. "It's OK. You're not the first person to believe in my dad and what he's offering. But take it from me, it isn't as easy as just changing your mind and walking out. Not with him."

"Sure it is," he says, and tries the locked front door. "He took my keys back earlier – he thought I was going to let you go. But as soon as he comes back, I'll tell him I'm going."

Does he not understand how Dad's mind works at all?

"You shouldn't wait," I say. "You and I can force this door or smash out a window together."

Before we can try anything at all, the lock rattles. Dad's back. He's sweaty from his run round the boundaries, still wearing his camo utility jacket and backpack.

"What's going on?" he says, looking from Will to me to the bags.

"I've decided to go, Mr Fitzpatrick," says Will. "This isn't what I signed up for, Ellis. You were meant to be creating a better way of life – not this."

"I see." Dad nods his head and rubs his chin as though he's carefully considering Will's point of view. I know the fake routine. "If you want to go, go. You've got five seconds to get off my land."

"What? It's not even your land, see," says Will, laughing slightly. "You're borrowing it. Remember? And I don't think other preppers are going to like what you're doing here any more than I do."

Dad picks up his baseball cap and fixes it firmly on his head as he begins counting. "One."

"Don't worry, I'm going anyway. But Amber's coming with me." He holds out his hand to me. "Come on."

"Two. Amber's not going anywhere. She belongs to me." Dad's calm. He takes off his backpack and kicks the mud from his trainers.

I take one step towards Will. But I know Josh is still in the basement. If I go now, what happens to him? And walking away from my dad, running, *hiding* from him hasn't ever solved anything for me. I need to face that head-on.

"Three. Stay right there, Amber." Dad undoes his backpack and draws out his hunting rifle.

"For fuck's sake! What the hell are you doing?" says Will, edging towards the door. "You've lost it, mate."

Dad attaches the scope and clicks the catch into place. "Are you too stupid to understand counting? Four." He raises the weapon and points it at Will.

"Go!" I mouth at him.

He grabs his bags and rushes through the open door into the darkness.

"Five," says Dad, and fires the gun up into the sky. He marches out of the door, reloading as he goes, footsteps crunching on the gravel.

I follow. I don't like the look in his eyes. The fixed stare.

"Dad – no more!"

Will sprints off towards the trees. He abandoned his bags after the first shot. He's fit, fast. Once he gets to the darkness and the cover of the woods, he'll be OK.

Dad fires the gun again.

Will ducks then zigzags across the grass. The strips on his coat glint in the moonlight.

"Run, Will," I say under my breath.

"I told you to get off my land in five seconds," screams Dad. "You broke a Rule. *Never break the Rules.*" He raises the rifle to his shoulder and looks through the night-vision scope. A shot rings out.

Will drops to the ground.

Dad shot him. In the back. On a five-second warning.

I don't make a sound. Both hands rush to cover my mouth, but no noise comes out.

Dad runs towards Will and I follow, stumbling my way behind him. Dad gets to Will, circling, with the rifle still pointed at him, and pushes at his body with his foot. He bends to take a pulse on his neck and lowers his ear to his face and chest, listening for breathing.

My legs are weak. I edge closer to them. To Will's body, slumped a metre from the trees. I can't tell if he's still alive. I can't see if his chest is rising and falling. I want to heave. I've never seen so much blood. It's seeping across the back of his shirt, spilling into the ground. I gag, turning to throw up behind me.

"Is-is he OK?" I stutter, wiping my mouth on the back of my hand. My voice sounds thin, like a young child intruding on an adult scene. I've never seen a dead human being before. Not a real one. A piece of engineered metal and a tiny bullet have taken down Will, a living breathing person. I know the answer to my own foolish question. Will is far from OK. "Dad? Daddy?" I tug at his sleeve.

But he doesn't answer at first. He takes a long moment staring down at Will before he turns to me, like he's surprised to see me here. The blood on his hands is bright red: Will's blood.

"We need to go," he says.

You can't just shoot people and leave them to die in the woods. And yet he is. *We* are. Dad doesn't even seem that bothered. It's like he'd fired at a deer on a hunting trip. He reloads.

"We need to get help for him, for Will," I say quietly, but as firmly as I dare. "It's serious, Dad. He'll bleed to death. I'll get the first-aid kit. But I can't treat a gunshot wound on my own."

Dad chews on his lip.

"If he dies, it'll be worse. The police will come," I say. "The state will be here, asking questions, crawling over the house, the land. They'll stop the Ark."

"You're wrong," he says. "No one's going to miss that piece of nothing. He wasn't following the Rules, Amber. *Don't break the Rules.*"

"Do you have an emergency phone hidden somewhere? A satellite phone? A CB radio." They're not in the basement store – I looked thoroughly.

"We're not calling anyone."

"Dad, we can't just leave him. Look at him. How will you live with yourself?"

"I think we'll manage, don't you?"

What kind of a person leaves someone like that? I swallow hard. I already know.

He's thinking something through. I recognize the furrowed brows and the distant stare. I wait for him to do the right thing. To think it's his own idea to call an ambulance, not mine. But the relief is short-lived. He bends down again and checks Will's neck for a pulse. I force myself to look at his lifeless face in the moonlight. The eyes are half-closed, staring up at the starry sky but seeing nothing.

"There's no point calling anyone. He's gone. We'll have to bring it forwards, thanks to Will. He's ruined everything."

Not the Ark... "What? Now?"

"We'll have to start earlier, not wait until Christmas Eve."

No, no, no. "What about the others? Do we need to contact them, call someone?"

He turns and pushes me back towards the house.

"Wait. Should we cover him up? It's Will, Dad. Will!"

Dad grabs at my arm and pulls me along.

We're in the terrible finale to all this. Shooting Will dead has changed everything. What's the best I can hope for? Throwing myself out of the car? Wherever the Ark is – Scotland. Maybe back in Wales. The US? Wherever it is, he can't possibly plan an entire route where we see no one, never stop for fuel, never slow down. I'm breathing easier now I have a plan. *Stay one step ahead*, that's the Rule.

Dad twitches, wiping his sweaty forehead. And then he smiles at me. "No. That's the beauty of the Ark." He looks over his shoulder and pulls me closer towards him, leaving a bloody handprint on my sleeve. He lowers his voice until it's just a whisper. "It's right here. The Ark's right here, Amber." He places a slightly shaking finger on his lips.

"It can't be."

"Fooled you, didn't I?" He laughs as my car plan shatters into pieces and falls away into the darkness. He's leaving me no choices.

The Ark can't be here at Centurion House. It's not possible. I'm trying to get the logical part of my brain ticking through the options. He's shown me plans. Photographs. The surroundings were not like here. How could something of that size even fit on this land – the house, a couple of outbuildings and maybe five acres of boggy grass and some woods?

I saw the picture with the Joshua tree, the shrubland that was more like desert than here. I thought it was somewhere like Utah or Arizona.

What about the cooling stacks, the ventilation shafts? He's talked about a biodome, growing food on a hydroponic farm. He said a hundred people would be living there eventually.

Dad sighs and adjusts the gun. He'll have to put it down at some point but he's keeping it charged and ready.

Stay one step ahead. I'm a prepper. And the shit has hit the fan. Dad's armed.

"I need my Grab-and-Go Bag," I say.

He hesitates. "The Ark is fully equipped."

"*Always have your Grab-and-Go Bag*, right? It's a Rule." My boots crunch on the twigs while I wait for his answer, willing him to agree.

"*Never break the Rules.*" He sounds like a computer, an automaton.

He just shot Will. A living, breathing person.

As we go back into the house, my mind's whirring. The car plan is dead in the water so what's next? I need to tell Josh where Dad's taking me – ready for Neville's cavalry in the morning. Where *is* Dad taking me? Will he wait for other preppers to join us in the Ark?

My eyes flick to the advent calendar on the shelf. It's the twenty-first of December. If others are coming here for lockdown on Christmas Eve, they should be arriving soon, getting ready. They might arrive in the next few hours – they'll see Will's body. Except, as I pick up the advent calendar and look at all the doors that are open already,

I can't stop myself wondering why no one else is here already. Where *are* all the other people?

"I'm getting a fresh battery," says Dad, heading for the kitchen. "Make sure you put your head torch on. Hurry up."

I take a pen and write quickly on the back of the advent calendar that Dad shot Will dead by the trees and to stay in the basement quietly or Dad will shoot him too. I write in clear capitals that he's taking me against my will to the Ark nearby but I don't know where. I want to say more, to tell Josh more, but I can hear Dad coming back.

I post the advent calendar quickly under the basement door, pushing it as far as I can and hoping that Josh will see it and drag himself to reach it. With my ear to the door, I hear nothing. I toy with unlocking it. But it's best if Josh stays down there, sleeping off his painkillers and the alcohol. Unseen, unheard. Alive.

Today's advent window revealed a star, shining bright. Illuminating the way for those who seek an answer. Showing the way.

Dad comes back into the hall with the batteries. And the gun. "Amber? What's keeping you?"

"It's nearly midnight," I say. "Maybe it'd be best to wait until the morning."

He pulls repeatedly at his ear and mutters, "No, no, no." Why can't he wash his hands at least, change his clothes? Will's blood is slowly drying from fresh red to rust-colour.

"We have to go now," he says agitated. "Will ruined everything. It's his fault that we need to bring it forwards. We need to go now."

I pick up my Grab-and-Go Bag and take a last glance at the hall and the door to the basement. There are no sounds. Dad switches on his head torch and I do the same.

He leads me round the back of the house, takes the gate behind the oil tank that leads down towards the paddock and the old barn. It's beginning to snow. Gentle flakes stick to my lashes and melt on my cheeks. He's muttering to himself but nothing that makes any sense. There's nothing here. Is he just going to shoot me in the woods, like Will?

"You'll see, Amber. You'll see the future. Hiding in plain sight," he whispers. "Always the best way. Because they are always watching us, always looking. Never forget you are being watched."

"It's dark, Dad."

He pulls me down into a crouching position while he scans the area with the rifle scope. "What if they are watching us now? What if there's a drone? They have thermal imaging. They can pick up your body heat. Crawl."

Everything he says is stupid, illogical, irrational. But Will had twice my strength and couldn't stop Dad shooting him so I bide my time. Dad always said that a bullet doesn't distinguish between the types of flesh it slices through. I play along with his commando game.

There are no drones. The sky is heavy with stars.

The most I've ever seen. Completely and utterly beautiful.

We crawl through the damp grass in the paddock until we reach the barn and he pulls me to my feet. He draws a keyring from his pocket and selects a normal key. I was expecting a big entrance – like in his pictures – a concrete ramp leading to an underground silo. A blast door, a keypad, cameras – where is it all?

He fumbles with the lock on the old barn.

Is there a passageway inside? A concealed set of steps? I'm impressed.

"You're the first to see it, Amber. Only you. You're my flesh and blood. Blood's thicker than water. It was only ever for you." He catches sight of the blood on his hands and looks puzzled. He wipes them on his trousers than holds out his hand to me.

"At last we can live by the Rules. I was right all along, Amber. It's me who's right, isn't it? Not them. Not your mom. Not people like Will. No one knows better than me. *I am the Rules and the Rules are me.*"

"Sure, Dad. Living by the Rules. You and me. For ever and ever."

I keep my hands by my sides. I don't take his. Will's blood is crusted on his fingernails in the torchlight. He points the rifle in my direction and I shuffle forwards.

The door shudders open.

Dad says, "Welcome to the Ark."

The door catches on the ground where one of the slats

protrudes. The floor is just dirt. I jolt to one side as a pigeon flies out of the door in a flap of wings. My eyes adjust as Dad pushes me in and locks the door behind us. I turn my head torch from one side to another.

White lines mark out a strange set of squares on the floor. A ladder stands by the back wall, next to open cans of paint and creosote. He's been busy. It's like the wall back at Eden Farm, but bigger. Painted in giant letters, drips running down the wall, blending one line into another. Words misspelt, repeated. Random capital letters thrown in.

The Rules.

I look again at the lines on the floor and I realize what it is. A floor plan, badly measured out in the dirt, roughly like the plan he showed me the other day. The plan of the Ark.

Dad's practically bouncing with excitement while I'm rooted to the spot with shock. My brain's struggling to find an explanation, to join the dots in some way other than the obvious.

There is no Ark.

There never will be.

It's all in his head.

No one else is coming.

There is no one else.

"What do you think?" he asks, his eyes wide. He's like a child. A child showing me the castle he's made from sticks and an old blanket. "Here's the plant room I told you about. We can produce so much electricity from the solar panels and the heat-exchange pump and the windmills. We'll never want for anything."

I swallow. I close my eyes for a moment then reopen them. Nothing has changed. A load of farm junk. Dented gas canisters.

"Where are the windmills, Dad? The wind turbines?"

He laughs. "Not in here, silly. Out there. In rows on the hillside. Hundreds and hundreds of them. We can survive here for years and years. Just you and me. We don't need anyone else."

He leads me down the corridor marked on the floor in tiny steps. "And this is our apartment. I reserved us the best spot."

We stand in a marked-out white box about four metres square. The only contents are bird poo and debris from the nesting pigeons cooing above us. A small hole in the wall that they must use as an entrance lets in a circle of weak moonlight to pool on the floor of 'my room'.

Dad points out the features – the features in the rooms in the glossy pictures and plans back on the table at Centurion House. Our private kitchen area is marked by a long-dead baby bird, right next to an old can which he calls a control panel to operate the daylight pipes and the ventilation system.

"Where's the food store, Dad?" You know, the refrigerated room, the freezers run by generators, the dried-goods store?

The hydroponic containers? Where's all the food, the crops already growing for the future? The seed store?

All the lies you told me. That I believed. That Will believed. That he died for.

Dad leads me to the far corner of the building. A few cans and jars sit on an old oil stain on a ripped tarpaulin. "Unpack your supplies," he says. "We've got provisions to last for years. Just you and me now."

I arrange the food, following the Rule: *Everything has its place. Cans and jars should face forwards and be exactly one centimetre apart.*

Sets of clothes should be laid out in order, ready to put on in an emergency. I lay my clothes in the correct piles in my 'bedroom', ready to wear, trying to calm myself with the routine.

Dad seems happier than he has in days, humming to himself as he watches my preparations.

There's an empty mixing bucket in the pile of junk by the ladder. I take it to the chalk-drawn 'bathroom'. He seems pleased. Is it a bath, sink, toilet, bucket? Deluxe hot tub? I don't know what the hell he's seeing. I find the anti-bacterial gel and the toilet roll in my bag. Are we staying here? Am I making myself an actual prison toilet?

He takes me round the rest of the Ark – pointing out the giant biodome in the corner. He genuinely sees it. He steps gingerly past the rows of vegetables, tells me not to squash any. I find myself looking at the ground, picking my way carefully over the dirt and loose stones in case I ruin his imaginary pumpkins. "We'll save the rest of the tour for tomorrow and the daylight. Wait till you see the water filtration system."

His enthusiasm makes me doubt my own eyes. Do I not *believe* in it enough to see it?

Then it's like he's reached into my head and read what I'm thinking. "You just had to believe in me, Amber. You just had to believe."

"Poor Will…" I start to say. He wanted something better out of life and this is what he'd have got. What a waste.

"He didn't follow the Rules," says Dad. He taps his finger on his nose and says in a sing-song voice, *"Don't break the Rules!"*

He drags over a couple of ancient heaters, stinking of dust and fumes as he sets them working. He sits down cross-legged in the 'atrium' area amongst the pigeon poo and surveys the wall, muttering a disjointed set of Rules. He checks the catch on the gun and lays it across his knees like a banjo.

I'm floating above the scene, struggling to grasp some reality. "Shall I start a fire? Make food?" someone in my body says.

"It's his own fault, Amber," he says. He repeats it like he's trying to convince himself he hasn't just murdered a teenage boy. "I made a new Rule today," he says. "I told Will, but he didn't want to follow it." He shakes his head sadly.

I'm holding my breath. My whole body is straining to see the words he's scratching in the dirt with the end of the rifle.

RULE: THERE'S NO WAY OUT.

RULE:
KILL OR BE KILLED

I hated those caves at Eden Farm. Hated the so-called
bunker. Hated *him*.

Dark.

So dark.

The lights flickered on and off,

on and off.

Off.

Scratching rats lived in the caves. A tail flicked across my
flesh in the darkness and I screamed and lashed out.

I held a candle, shaking, watching it burn slowly down as
I ate from a can of peaches.

The toilet smelled foul. The chemicals merged with the
stench of wee and poo and vomit.

Was it a day – or a week – a month – or an hour? Time
both stood still and raced up and down, until I had no

concept of it at all.

With no day and night, no watch, no calendar.

I just wanted to know what day it was.

The date.

Never-ending.

I read my notes with the last blast of candlelight.

My captain's log.

My prison diary.

I HATE HIM
I HATE HIM
I HATE HIM

Written on page after page.

I HATE HIM.

The candle died.

Part of me died.

A key in the lock, the squeak of iron gates, a handle turning.

A flicker of lights, of a video camera clicking into action.

A rock lifted high above my head in shaking hands.

Gravity brought it down. Not me. Not my hands. No.

The rock came down with a sickening crack of bone and tissue.

He slumped.

All reflected in an unblinking camera's eye.

I ran.

I left him like that.

I ran away.

I ran to Mum.

Mum made me swear to keep the secret.

Secrets are heavy.

Even if you try to keep moving on.

The secrets of what I'd done. Of what I was.

I feared I'd killed the monster in the cave.

I hoped I'd killed the monster in the cave.

Who was the monster? Me or him?

December
22

Dad sits hunched by the fire we've made in the centre of the Ark, shivering even though he's sitting way too close to the flames. The gun is still in his hands – his finger trembles on the trigger. The combination of burning wood and fumes from the extra heaters is choking.

"Write up the new Rule," he says again and gestures to the ladder, tall and rickety. For Dad, his latest edict doesn't properly exist until it's been added to the scrawl of the others.

"When everything is in its place," I say, tidying away our meal of a can of peaches. Snack? Supper? Breakfast? It doesn't matter.

I'm calm.

Resolved.

I know what I must do.

This is my new reality. With Dad till the end. Following the Rules. It's the only way. I should never have resisted.

I finish unpacking my Grab-and-Go Bag, putting my last items where they need to be, while Dad mutters on about Will and stares at the blood on his hands like Macbeth, his eyes half closing.

He barely acknowledges me or my voice now as I climb the ladder in the darkness, struggling with the open paint pot. My feet slip on the rungs as I edge my way to the very top. The candles flicker as I look down. Dad's enclosed in a circle of lights, bright against the dark earth. A stage set.

I paint the new Rule on the wall. The last Rule. Slowly, carefully. Doing the job in the best way I can. Like he taught me. Everything is as he taught me.

"There, Daddy. See. *Rule: There's no way out.* Just as you wanted."

All is calm, my voice is muffled. He doesn't reply. I wait.

I edge my way back down the ladder, breathing heavily, my face hot and clammy. I look back up at the sprawling handwriting, the curve of the brush, the words large enough to read from the ground.

I admire my handiwork.

My father is quiet. His eyes are closed, his head slumped. He doesn't appreciate my craftsmanship.

I tidy up. I add logs to the fire.

He looks uncomfortable. I give him a jumper to use as a cushion.

And carefully, oh-so-carefully, I remove the key from his pocket, ready to release myself from the Ark, back into the real world.

———

The first hints of orange light are prickling the horizon. It's the winter solstice – the shortest day of the year. The sun won't rise until half eight. The morning reveals a scattering of snow and my torch picks out trees from a Christmas-card scene. My boots crunch on the snow in the quiet, making the first footprints through the paddock. Like I've stepped into a picture, through the advent-calendar door.

As I reach the house, I half hope that what happened to Will can't be real – that it's not possible when the world looks so beautiful. But his dead body, now with a layer of decorative white frosting, still lies unmoving by the trees. I look away.

I need to let Josh out. I brace myself for the stream of questions. Prepare myself to break my silence, to have to talk again, to speak.

His first few words don't register. He's concerned for me, my cuts and bruises, he's relieved that I'm OK. I nod but don't really hear him as I help him up the stairs. He's made a makeshift crutch from a broom, proud of his ingenuity. "I'm getting the hang of this prepper business," he jokes weakly. I check my watch. "I opened your advent calendar. Didn't think you'd mind. A Christmas cracker going bang.

Seems pretty trivial after what your dad did, Will didn't deserve that."

I tune him out, focus on getting him up and out of the house.

"Amber!" He's looking me straight in the face, demanding an answer. Interaction. "Amber, you're not listening. Where's your dad now?"

"Sleeping. In the barn."

"Where's the gun?"

"He's not going to shoot anyone again."

"You won't mind if we get out of here before we put your theory to the test? Here's hoping Neville set his alarm clock and made that call."

I help him out of the house, the door still thrown wide open from my arrival. He sniffs at the air. "Is that … burning?"

We turn the corner, looking out across the paddock. I stand transfixed, my hands cupped across my face. Josh gasps. The barn is ablaze, clouds of flame and smoke billowing from the roof. Flames are licking from the doorway, a giant beacon lighting up the early-morning countryside. A couple of explosions send sparks up into the morning sky. "Shit," says Josh. "Your dad. Is he in there?

I make my legs move. I dash back down to the basement, grabbing a fire extinguisher from the shelves. I run across the field, towards the searing heat. Josh is shouting behind me, "Amber! No! It's too dangerous!"

He doesn't want me to try to put the fire out. Doesn't want me to risk myself. He's using his crutch to hobble closer too, to drag me back. I cough and pull my jumper up over my mouth and nose.

"Amber! It's hopeless."

The heat is overwhelming. The noise. Cracks and hisses and pops. Another canister ignites with a bang and a section of the wooden building blows out.

"Amber! Get back!"

The fire extinguisher is empty already. Even the patch I sprayed by the doorway flares up again, the heat unbearable against my skin. It's made no difference.

The Ark is a living, hissing ball of fire.

Josh is grabbing my arms, pulling me back, pulling me far away. We tumble down into the cold grass at the far edge of the field. "Enough," he says, wrapping his arms round me. "Think of yourself."

I am.

The fire is raging.
It's majestic.

Apocalyptic.

I stretch out my legs in the waiting area at the police station and pick at the corner of the dressing that covers the burns on the back of my hand. I'm tired of going over the same story again and again in hushed-tone interviews. Doctors, police, social workers, chaplains. Repeat. Repeat. All with the same pitying looks for me. The same words whispered: ordeal – trauma – shocking – brave – victim. Endless do-gooders with their lanyards hanging round their necks like backstage passes – they all want a piece of me.

The paramedics treated me and Josh at Centurion House, sirens blaring as the barn still blazed in the paddock. They wrapped us in shiny foil shrouds. But it didn't stop me shaking. From just the two of us curled up in the paddock on the snowy ground to police cars and fire engines and ambulances and so many people.

All prepared for emergency.

They helped us get our things from the house and led us to the ambulance. Black ash swirled across the terrace and caught in my hair and throat. The fire fighters were dampening down what was left of the barn.

And Dad.

We drove out past the solemn ring of uniforms around Will's body. A different sort of ambulance was called for him.

At the hospital, a kindly doctor said I'll need a lot of time to process what I've suffered. I nodded. I cried. I took the offered tissues. The shoulder to cry on.

We got off lightly. Everyone said so. A touch of smoke inhalation, minor burns, cuts and bruises. Fading already after a night in a crisp-sheeted hospital bed. Even Josh's ankle will soon be mended. Physical injuries are easy to patch up.

But some things you never get over.

They're following their procedures, their rules. My words are treated reverently by the police and arranged into neat pages of statements for their files. Ready for the truth to be paraded when the inquests come, to be relayed to Will's weeping mother.

Rev Neville nods over at me and Josh as he's ushered into another interview room. "I'll be taking us home after this one, Josh. Promise." His smile's still wonky on his swollen face, but he's here to play his part.

The family liaison officer nudges my arm. "Touch of divine intervention from that vicar, eh?" she says. "Good job he called 999 and got the emergency services to you. A place as remote as that, the fire wouldn't have been seen."

"But they were too late to put it out," I say. "Too late to..." I cough slightly as I stare down at my injured hands.

I've had enough of talking now but she mistakes my silence and adds, "You certainly tried your hardest to save your father. No one can say otherwise. Even though he'd..." Her sentence trails off as she thinks better of spelling it out. Even though he'd what? Murdered Will. Imprisoned me at gunpoint. Been the survivalist who didn't survive when the shit really did hit the fan.

"And you a tiny slip of a lass, as well. Could have been a lot worse for a hero like you than a night in hospital, eh?" She fetches me another lukewarm drink in a plastic cup. It's been her answer to all uncomfortable silences today. She's called away and leaves me to contemplate the swirling coffee.

Josh is uncharacteristically quiet. I guess even he gets tired of repeating the same thing. "Divine intervention – is that what it was?" he says. He flicks through the magazines on the table, not settling to read anything properly.

The sympathetic officer is back, clutching my sorry bag of belongings. "Got someone who's come to collect you. Drink up while we get through the paperwork. After all you've been through, pet, we'll get you out of here as soon as."

I recognize her footsteps before I see her – those sensible shoes of hers that squeak on the tiled floor. Julie's wearing a ridiculous knitted hat with earflaps and a padded duvet jacket that looks like an actual king-size duvet with sleeves. It does her no favours. Except that, when she envelops me in the soft, pillowy warmth of it, I crumple into its folds.

When I turn back, after fielding all her questions about how I'm feeling, the chairs are empty. Josh is gone. His back is disappearing through the swing doors. I leave Julie to her expertise with bureaucracy and hurry after him.

"Josh! Josh! I'm going in a minute."

"I'm not big on goodbyes," he says, not meeting my eyes. "Going to get me and Neville a sandwich for the journey back." He turns away but I pull at his arm.

"I wanted to say thanks. For coming back to help me."

He shrugs. "I tried to help you. But I think you pretty much had it all in hand." He pulls awkwardly at the new clothes Neville had brought him, too small for his long limbs.

"Thanks anyway," I say. "For everything. And for, you know, the statements you gave about yesterday." We look into each other's eyes until I pull away. "If ever you need a sofa to sleep on or someone to play bus roulette with, let me know."

"Amber – I wouldn't blame you. I get it," he says, his voice barely a whisper.

I screw up my face in puzzlement. "I don't know what you mean." I reach up and hug him. "We're practically family, right?"

"I said I've got your back. I always will, Amber Warning. Whatever."

Julie calls me from down the corridor, "Amber, love! Time to go."

I give Josh one last quick squeeze. "Be careful with that bullshit monitor of yours."

———

"You're going to be all right, you know," Julie says. "You're one of life's survivors, Amber. Always have been."

As usual, the irony is lost on Julie. I am a survivor in more ways than one. A prepper. At least, I used to be. I place my few belongings in Julie's boot, keeping only one thing to hand.

"Sorry I've mucked up your Christmas, Julie," I say.

She chews on her lip. Unable to tell an outright lie. "That doesn't matter. Anyway, a wise person once told me that Christmas is just a day when the shops are shut and the telly's better." She smiles over at me and the corners of my mouth twitch up too. I can't help it.

She checks her phone and jots something down in her stripey notebook. "I've got it cleared with the powers that be," she says. "Want to come back with me for a few days and watch some telly?"

I nod.

"If I put my foot down, we should be back in time for Christmas Eve," she says as she squeezes into the driver's seat.

I sit in the passenger seat beside her and fasten my seat belt.

"Dad had money," I say quietly. "I'd like to sort out a headstone. Despite … everything."

A pause while Julie processes 'despite everything'. He was hardly a candidate for father of the year. But he was still my father. My flesh and blood.

She nods. "Of course. I can help with all that. No need to worry about it now. Whatever you want, sweetie," she says, patting my knee.

Yes. Whatever *I* want.

Julie crunches through the gears, manoeuvring out of the car park. A tall, gangly figure in a green parka jacket, hood up, is leaning against the wall. He raises one of his hospital-issue crutches in goodbye.

"You'll be in the spare room," Julie says. "I decorated it this summer. It's pink."

My least favourite colour. Why am I not surprised? It'll be full of frills and polyester.

But I so want to sleep in a normal bed. In a normal house. For a million years.

First though I'll lay out what's left of my clothes in the correct way. *Sets of clothes should be laid out in order, ready to put on in an emergency.*

Because everything has its place. Even me.

I am the Rules and the Rules are me.

I unfold my crumpled advent calendar and rest it in my

lap. I pull off today's door to show a candle with a flickering flame.

"Oh, you kept that with you all the time. That's so lovely." Julie's cheeks tinge red.

I've made her happy.

"Just tomorrow's door left to open," she says. "The biggest one of all."

RULE:
NEVER BREAK THE RULES

Carbon monoxide is a silent killer.

Heavier than air.

It kills the man with a gun sitting on the floor before the girl at the top of the ladder.

THE ONLY USEFUL KNOWLEDGE IS THE STUFF THAT KEEPS YOU ALIVE.

I failed with the mushrooms.

I failed with the rock.

Third time lucky.

THE ENDS JUSTIFY THE MEANS.

Air-supply respirators work well for carbon monoxide

emissions.

I did my research.

PREP FOR THE WORST.

I replaced my mask in my bag.

ALWAYS HAVE YOUR GRAB-AND-GO BAG.

I tidied up.

I pulled out my clothes that were rammed tight inside any ventilation holes and packed them neatly away.

EVERYTHING HAS ITS PLACE.

I gave him a pillow. I placed his arms across his chest and said goodbye.

HONOUR THY FATHER.

I removed the key from his pocket and walked out of the Ark.

STAY ONE STEP AHEAD.

I put a bruise on my face and a cut on my lip with a deft, swift strike with a log. Just the right amount of force to bruise but not to hurt too much. I *am* trained in hand-to-hand combat.

KILL OR BE KILLED.

I plaited my hair while I waited for the dawn because it made me look more innocent.

Blame the patriarchy for that.

USE YOUR WEAKNESS AS YOUR STRENGTH.

The fire? Well, that was bound to happen. The Ark was a health-and-safety nightmare. The footage from Eden was destroyed in the fire with everything else I left there.

LEAVE NO TRACE.

A mixture of paint and gas canisters is dangerous in a confined space. Throw in a couple of paraffin and butane heaters, candles, ammunition, logs on an open fire and – whoosh!

Physics and chemistry combined.

THERE'S NO WAY OUT.

The facts spoke for themselves.

Will's slowly stiffening dead body in the bushes was

more eloquent than me in my distress.

I had a sympathetic witness who loves to talk.

One who never shuts up.

Josh saw me take a fire extinguisher from the basement store, saw me run to try to save my dad.

I was the hero in this story.

But it was all too late. Dad didn't follow the Rules.

NEVER BREAK THE RULES.

I AM THE RULES AND THE RULES ARE ME.

I'm not a monster.

I'm a survivor.

SURVIVAL IS EVERYTHING.

TRUST NO ONE.

Including me.

DISCUSSION QUESTIONS

1. Amber says at the very end that she was the hero in this story. Do you agree?

2. Did you like Amber at the beginning of the novel? If so, did you still like her at the end? Does it matter if a character is likeable or not? Can you still feel empathy for them?

3. Why are people like Will drawn to the Rules and to a character like Amber's father?

4. Could a society based on the Rules ever succeed?

5. Do you think that constantly dwelling on disaster could have a major emotional effect?

6. Should we all be acquiring skills or kit for after a SHTF scenario?

7. Amber says her mum became a shadow. How did that happen?

8. Do you believe that Amber can ever escape her upbringing?

9. What are your thoughts about the way Josh lives his life? Is it by choice or circumstance?

10. Do you think Josh felt used at the end? Will he and Amber see each other again?

11. Did Amber take an active role in her dad's death, or did she let it happen without trying hard enough to stop it? Does that alter your view of her guilt and responsibility?

12. Look at the structure of the story: a present storyline mirroring the opening of the advent calendar with flashback sections based around the Rules. Why was it told in this way rather than chronologically?

13. When is it OK to break rules? What about breaking the law – can it ever be justified?

ACKNOWLEDGEMENTS

Biggest thank you of all to my amazing editor Ruth Bennett, ably assisted by Ella Whiddett.

The brilliant team at Stripes – Lauren Ace, Charlie Morris, Leilah Skelton – and to Sophie Bransby for such a striking cover. And to lovely copyeditor Anna Bowles.

My agent Jo Williamson for being all-round fab and supportive.

Those who helped me with some of my research – Angela, Callen, Craig, Mark, Helen and Hugh.

Writing buddies from the Bath Spa MA gang and beyond who continue to help and support.

My crit groups – the Rogue Critters and the Teaspooners.

And especially my beta readers James, Ally, Emma, Ele, Karen, Mel, Christine, Tricia and Pete.

To my long-suffering and sadly neglected friends who

drag me away from my desk to the real world, and who've always got my back.

To my goddaughter Hannah W whose cheerleading gave me a boost just when I needed it.

To all those readers, bloggers, booksellers and librarians who've kindly told me that they loved *The Truth About Lies*, thank you. And a special shout-out to supportive librarian extraordinaire Kevin Sheehan and my #BookPenPals at Poynton High School.

Lastly, to Dolf and my boys James and Ally whose enthusiasm for taking me on adventures and wild camping has finally paid off.

Writing books is hard. *The Rules* wouldn't have happened without *all* of you.

ABOUT THE AUTHOR

Tracy Darnton is an award-winning author of books for children and young people. Her debut novel, *The Truth About Lies*, was shortlisted for the Waterstones Children's Book Prize. Tracy studied law at Cambridge and worked as a solicitor and law lecturer before enrolling on the Bath Spa MA Writing for Young People, from which she graduated with Distinction. Amber from *The Rules* first appeared in Tracy's short story, 'The Letter', for which she won the Stripes YA Short Story Prize, run in partnership with The Bookseller's YA Book Prize, and was published in the YA anthology *I'll Be Home for Christmas*. Tracy lives in Bath with her husband and two sons – and a large Grab-and-Go Bag.

@TracyDarnton